Books by J.M. Hayes

Mad Dog and Englishman Mysteries
Mad Dog & Englishman
Prairie Gothic
Plains Crazy
Broken Heartland
Server Down

Other Mysteries
The Grey Pilgrim

Server Down

Server Down

A Mad Dog & Englishman Mystery

J.M. Hayes

Poisoned Pen Press

Poisoned
Pen
Press

First Edition 2009

10 9 8 7 6 5 4 3 2 1

Library of Congress Catalog Card Number: 2008937733

ISBN: 978-1-59058-627-3 Hardcover

Poisoned Pen Press
6962 E. First Ave., Ste. 103
Scottsdale, AZ 85251
www.poisonedpenpress.com
info@poisonedpenpress.com

Printed in the United States of America

For Phi Beta Kimba,
guardian of the gate,
protector of the family,
forever, part of my soul

I believe that the flag
It was more than a rag
But the outlaws in office
Have shattered my life.
—John Stewart (1939–2008)
"Survivors"

Author's Note:

Buffalo Springs and Benteen County, Kansas are fictitious. Tucson, though it should be, is not. In the same vein, the Sewa tribe, its police force, and reservation are inventions. Pascua Yaqui Village is real, as is its habit of sharing the intimacies of ancient ceremonies with people willing to view them with respect.

The echo of drums and softly chanting voices didn't help Pascua resemble an Indian village. It was a drab cluster of municipal buildings surrounded by a mixed neighborhood—nice-but-modest homes and industrial-urban blight. Still, a five-hundred-year-old ceremony was taking place there. That made it beautiful, and worth the thousand mile drive.

Mad Dog parked his Mini Cooper across the street. He looked at his watch and smiled. Midnight. The drive had taken a bit less than sixteen hours and gotten him no speeding tickets.

Hailey stuck her muzzle in his ear and whined. The massive wolf-hybrid had been a surprisingly docile passenger. Now, she wanted out. He leaned over and opened the passenger door and she launched herself into the dusty lot beside his parking space.

He opened his own door and stepped onto broken asphalt through which a few weeds protruded. He stretched muscles, cramped from occupying too small a space for too many hours, then walked around to the back of the car. He opened the hatch, and pulled out Hailey's bowl and a jug of water. He put most of the jug in her bowl, then drained the last himself. Neither of them had drunk much today. He'd wanted to avoid pit stops and make good time and Hailey had seemed to understand. She'd curled up on the back seat and slept most of the way. Until he pulled up here, a few blocks east of I-10 in Tucson, she hadn't complained. She'd just taken advantage of the stops he'd made and never once gone off exploring. Now, silver coat gleaming in the reflection of a bright moon and distant street lamps, she bounded back and helped herself to a generous drink. By the time Mad Dog put the jug back in the Mini, she'd disappeared.

The air was warm, at least compared with where he'd come from. And heavy with the perfume of blooming things. Citrus, maybe. The thermometer had still been under thirty degrees when he left home that morning. It must be at least seventy here, even if it wasn't yet April.

Hailey didn't reappear, so he locked the hatch and put her water bowl by the passenger door. He left the window on her side down in case she wanted back in. Most people would have been concerned if their pet jumped out of a car a thousand miles from home and promptly vanished. Mad Dog wasn't. Hailey was no pet. She was much more and she could take care of herself anywhere.

Mad Dog left his jacket behind. He even rolled up his sleeves as he crossed the narrow street and slipped beneath scraggly trees, their branches dancing to a wind he had expected to leave on the Great Plains. It wasn't much of a breeze by Kansas standards. Back there, it sometimes seemed no more than a dozen trees and a handful of fence posts slowed its passage back and forth between the Gulf and the Arctic Ocean. Here, there were mountains. Even now, inside the city, he could make out the jagged bite they took out of the night sky.

He headed toward the sounds and the lights. Low voices. Chanting. Drums. Rattles. He stepped through a gate and into a different world.

Ahead of him was a church, open at the front, and facing a plaza. A host of crosses and dark-skinned people filled the space. Dim electric lights failed to match the illumination from roaring fires. Two processions, one of men, one of women, approached a cross. Around that cross, a horde of demons fought a confused battle. White-faced creatures with great ears and short horns battled beasts in Halloween-like masks. They all wore belts of rattles that made more noise than the cap guns they fired at each other. They cut and thrust and parried with wooden swords and daggers, too. It was wonderful. It was everything Mad Dog had hoped for. Everything his niece, Heather, had promised.

"Wow," Mad Dog whispered.

Someone grabbed his arm and swung him around. "*Brujo*," the man hissed. "Why are you here?"

"My name's not Brujo," Mad Dog said. "And take your hand off me."

"You cannot bring your evil to this holy place."

"What evil?" Mad Dog took the man's thumb and bent it back.

The stranger, a compact, dark-skinned man with long braided hair and a beaded head band, lost his grip, but he hissed that name again, "*Brujo!*" and swung at Mad Dog's face with his other hand. Mad Dog slipped the blow but the man got hold of Mad Dog's medicine pouch and tore it from his throat. There were precious things in there—ochre from the Cheyenne sacred mountain, a strand of hair from the girl who loved him, a tiny diamond his mother had worn in one of her ears.

Hailey was suddenly there, her mouth on the man's hand. Just holding it, so far, as she growled her threat to make further use of sharp teeth.

"What's going on here?" Another man joined them in the shadows by the gate. This one also had dark skin and high cheek bones, though his military-style short black hair was sprinkled with silver. He was in uniform and he kept one hand on the butt of his service revolver.

"This man attacked me."

It took Mad Dog a moment to realize that the right explanation had been offered, but by the wrong person.

"He tried to steal my medicine pouch and his dog bit me."

Mad Dog shook his head. "That's not true. It was the other way around. He's got my pouch right there in his hand."

"Just look at him," Mad Dog's accuser said. "You think some gringo is going to own a medicine pouch?"

"I'm Cheyenne," Mad Dog said. The cop seemed doubtful. Mad Dog knew he looked about as white as possible. He was big and broad and bald—bald because, when he'd tried to grow hair long enough for braids, it had come in with the kind of curls some women paid small fortunes to achieve. And light brown, or at least it used to be. It was more likely gray by now. He couldn't tell for sure because he shaved his head at least once every day.

"I think you better take your dog and go," the cop said. "Dogs aren't allowed."

"What dog?" Mad Dog said. Hailey had done another disappearing act. The moment the cop arrived, she'd faded into the night.

"I can tell you what's in that medicine pouch," Mad Dog added. "This guy can't because it's not his."

"Not true," the man with the braids said. "But it can't be opened. It's sacred. A holy thing. Open it and you'll ruin it."

The cop put out his hand. "Give it to me. Then both of you follow me. We're going to step out in the street, under that lamp over there where we have some light so I can figure out what to do with you."

"But…" Mad Dog began.

"We're going to stop creating a disturbance, gentlemen. This is a sacred ceremony." He put a hand on both their arms and escorted them through the exit.

"I just drove a thousand miles to see this," Mad Dog protested.

"Good for you. And maybe you can still watch it after we…."

The officer stopped, a surprised look on his face as he glanced down at the knife handle that suddenly protruded from his chest. He gurgled and stumbled and fell, and the man who'd stabbed him, the man with the braids, began shouting something in a language Mad Dog didn't understand. From the way some nearby men began looking at Mad Dog, he was pretty sure it was something like "Help me lynch this gringo because he just murdered a police officer."

There were hundreds of people in the courtyard. No more than a dozen with skin as pale as his. Mad Dog wanted to stay and defend himself. But Hailey disagreed. She was beside him again, baring her teeth at several men who'd moved to block him. They stepped aside and she fled through the gap. Mad Dog followed her example.

◇◇◇

"Who are the guys with the swords and the cap guns?" Heather English asked.

"Those are Chapayekas," Ms. Jardine said.

Heather was a small-town Kansas girl. Ms. Jardine had been, too, until she retired from teaching at Buffalo Springs Elementary School to start selling crystals in Tucson.

"And Chapayekas are…?" Heather asked.

"I hope I've got this right," Ms. Jardine said. "I haven't been to these ceremonies in years. If I remember, they're playing the role of the Roman guards at Jesus' tomb at the moment. The procession of women, they're coming to discover that Jesus has risen."

"This is amazing," Heather said. Uncle Mad Dog had taken her to Pow-Wows back home, but never anything as elaborate and involved as this. She had tried to call Mad Dog to tell him about it. His phone was busy so she gave up and just emailed him. "It's too bad I couldn't let Uncle Mad Dog know about this early enough for him to have time to get here."

"Mad Dog would love it," Ms. Jardine said. "Hey, I love it. Thanks for giving me an excuse to share the Yaqui Easter ceremonies with someone. I didn't realize how much I missed them."

Ms. Jardine looked the part of an aficionado of Native American ceremonies. Her hair hung over her shoulders in braids that sparkled with the crystals woven into them. She wore a squaw dress and moccasins and was draped with Indian silver and turquoise. She made Heather feel underdressed in her jeans, white blouse, and blue blazer.

It was pure chance that Heather had been available to share the event. She was about to complete her law degree at the University of Kansas. One of her professors had learned that retired Supreme Court Justice Sandra Day O'Connor, who now taught at the University of Arizona, would host a two-day seminar for a select group of women law students from across the country in Tucson this week. Heather had applied and been accepted. Heather's mother had been a teacher in Buffalo Springs, too. She and Ms. Jardine had been good friends. Acquaintances went without saying. Buffalo Springs was too small for them to have avoided knowing each other, but it had gone way beyond that. And Ms. Jardine had taught Heather. Though Heather's mother had passed away several years ago, the relationship remained strong and Ms. Jardine had offered Heather a place to stay while she attended the seminar.

Heather was so impressed with these ceremonies that she'd immediately contacted her sister, an anthropology grad student at Texas Tech, and her uncle. Or tried, in the latter case. She'd never managed to connect with Mad Dog and her sister had been unable to get away.

"What Cheyenne shaman wouldn't love this?" Heather wondered. Uncle Mad Dog really was Cheyenne. So was she. Her sister wasn't. Her sister was adopted, though they were related on her mother's side and looked enough alike to be twins. The bloodline was her father's. Heather's grandmother had claimed to be a Cheyenne half-breed. Genealogical research later showed that her Cheyenne half actually was made up of equal parts Sans Arc, Mexican Cowboy, Buffalo Soldier, and the Cheyenne she'd claimed. As for the shaman thing, well, Uncle Mad Dog occasionally seemed to know and do some pretty remarkable things. Some pretty weird ones, too.

The women were on the south side of the plaza, not far from the open mouth of the church. The structure had no east wall and, therefore, seemed more welcoming than most churches to Heather. Not that she'd gone inside. While these ceremonies took place, Ms. Jardine had explained they should stay out of the way and watch respectfully. And, most important, not take any pictures. The Yaquis welcomed visitors, but not photographs, tape recorders, or notebooks. What was happening here wasn't a Kodak moment.

They watched the Yaqui women throw confetti over the figure of Christ.

"This goes on all night," Ms. Jardine said. "But the climax is tomorrow, the day before Easter. The Gloria, they call it—a battle between good and evil."

"Yeah?" Heather was glad she wasn't flying home until Sunday.

"The evil Chapayekas line up and charge the church over and over until they're killed by flowers and confetti. We can come back for that, but I'm afraid I'm not up for an all-nighter. I need my sleep or I'll look older than time by morning."

Ms. Jardine hardly showed her age. Her hair was gray and there were crinkles around her eyes, but that was it.

"I hate to miss anything," Heather said, "but yeah, I'm dead on my feet."

They threaded through the crowd, being careful not to get in the way of any of the participants. It took several minutes to make it to the plaza's main entrance. It was blocked with yellow crime-scene tape. Mostly, anyway. The remaining space was occupied by a muscular Indian wearing a Sewa Indian Nation Police uniform. The flashing lights of an emergency vehicle lit the street behind him. EMTs crouched over another uniformed man lying on the ground just short of the curb.

"What's going on?" Heather asked.

The man didn't answer. "I need to see some IDs, ladies, before you can go."

Ms. Jardine produced her driver's license. Heather decided on a different approach.

The big man made a note of Jardine's information, but he took a long time studying Heather's.

"Kansas? You're a long way from home, Deputy English."

"Yes, I am."

Benteen County's Sheriff English, her father, had been injured in a wild shootout more than a year ago. He'd sworn his daughter in as a temporary deputy at the time. She'd been on the county's books ever since because his recovery had gone more slowly than hoped. In the interim, the county had been so short-handed they even paid her to work whenever she'd been able to come home from school for a weekend. Just minimum wage, though. Still, she got a kick out of being able to flash her badge. People looked at a deputy differently than they did a twenty-three year-old law student.

"So, what happened—" she tried again.

The policeman wrote her name and Benteen County contact information on his sheet. He took his time, but he finally answered.

"Somebody knifed one of our officers," he said as he handed her ID back. "We're looking for a big bald guy. You notice anybody like that around here tonight?"

Heather exchanged glances with Ms. Jardine. Big bald guy fit the description of her Uncle Mad Dog. But Mad Dog was still back in Central Kansas as far as Heather knew.

"No," Heather said. "We didn't see anybody like that."

The big cop nodded. "Okay. You can go. But if you remember anything that might be helpful, call us."

The women nodded. They edged out the gate and past the spot where blankets were being held up to keep people like them from ogling the body.

"There's a name etched on the knife handle," a voice said from behind the curtain. "Anybody know someone called Mad Dog?"

◇◇◇

"That you, Englishman?"

Sheriff English hated that nickname, though what could you expect once your brother started calling himself Mad Dog? The sheriff also thought it was a stupid question. His only remaining deputy, an incompetent bumbler who was most effective while at home and asleep, wouldn't be crawling from behind the wheel of the Benteen County Sheriff's Department's black and white with a walker.

"Yeah, it's me," the sheriff said, arranging the contraption so he could get around without falling flat on his face.

The chief of the local volunteer fire department stepped out of the chill night and into the glow of the cruiser's interior lights.

"We did what we could," the man said, his breath fogging. "I think we'll save the out buildings, but there weren't nothing left of the house."

All that remained of the structure was a series of small bonfires. The volunteers weren't paying much attention to them because they were still working on the flames licking at the garage door.

Other bonfires, smaller ones, burned fitfully all over the yard, evidence that the house hadn't just burned, it had exploded.

The sheriff's mouth felt dry and his breath came harder than normal. "What about my…?"

"Don't know. There's no sign of your brother or that wolf of his. Of course we ain't had a chance to sift through those ashes yet."

"He would have been here, this time of night," the sheriff said. Hell, in Benteen County, even on a Friday night, they rolled the sidewalks up at dusk. There was nowhere to go—no movies, no bowling alley. Hardly any bars, and Mad Dog didn't drink. Not recreationally, anyway. "Any idea what happened?"

"Now, there we got lucky," the chief said. "Billy Macklin stopped by soon after we got here. He said he was taking Dana Miller home, driving by Mad Dog's place just at the moment the place blew."

Billy Macklin was maybe twenty-one, now, and the son of a member of the Benteen County Board of Supervisors. And the sheriff thought Billy had more likely been parked with Dana Miller somewhere nearby. Though sex in parked cars was the one recreational activity young people in Benteen County could enjoy consistently—this time of the year, with the motor running to supply heat as well as a quick getaway in case someone happened to come along—the sheriff doubted Billy and Dana had been in each other's pants. Not that he thought they hadn't experimented together with their sexuality. They were just odd kids, both of them. Geniuses, for whom all the world seemed to be an ongoing experiment. If Billy and Dana were parked near

Mad Dog's place when it blew up, they were more likely dissecting a fresh road kill than trying out positions recommended by the *Kama Sutra* for back seats. Whatever, he was lucky to have a witness of any sort. There wasn't much traffic on these back roads late at night. For that matter, there wasn't much traffic anytime, with the county's population in steady decline.

"Billy says there weren't any flames before the explosion. Says the house was lit up, normal looking. And then it just erupted like it was hit by a cruise missile. He saw someone, back lit, running away. Someone who jumped in a pickup and sped off without lights. You don't suppose that could have been Mad Dog?"

The sheriff wanted to think so, but if it had been his brother the sheriff would have heard from him by now. And his brother didn't have a pickup.

"Not likely," the sheriff said. "And I've tried calling his cell. Goes right to his messages. I've left several."

The chief hung his head. "Damn! I am *so* sorry, Sheriff."

The guys fighting the garage door fire finally managed to extinguish it. One of them took an ax to what remained. The sheriff thought about telling him it wouldn't be locked, but it wasn't like the man was damaging anything that wasn't already ruined. Besides, the guy had probably been looking forward to chopping his way into something from the moment they got the call.

"Billy still here?" the sheriff asked.

"Nah. He's gone on home. Other than telling us what he saw, wasn't nothing he could do to help."

"Billy have any idea what kind of truck it was?" the sheriff asked.

"No, sir. Says him and Dana was scared and ducked down when it went by and didn't get a good look."

What *were* Billy and Dana doing out here at this hour? That was just one of many questions the sheriff would ask them when he got the chance.

"Hey Chief! Sheriff!" It was the guy with the ax, hollering across the ruin that was Mad Dog's yard. "The garage is empty. Mad Dog's Mini Cooper isn't in here."

◇◇◇

Mad Dog hadn't the foggiest idea what to do next. He shouldn't have run. But Hailey had led the way and he'd had bad feelings about staying. Still had them about going back, even worse now.

He aimed the Mini down the first major street he found and headed east, away from the freeway. Getting out of town wouldn't work. Sooner or later, he was going to have to turn himself in to law enforcement. Getting caught on the interstate, they'd think he was trying to get away from Tucson. It would make him look even guiltier than…well, it was hard to imagine how much guiltier he could look than he already did.

He came to an intersection with a major thoroughfare and turned south. It wasn't like he knew where he was going. He'd been through Tucson a couple of times on his way to visit the Pacific Ocean. He hadn't stopped, except for gas and a meal and, once, to spend the night in a motel. Or had that been Benson or Gila Bend? He couldn't remember.

What he'd seen of the city so far had a surprisingly dim and industrial feel to it. Of the desert, there was no sign—except there were almost no patches of grass and damn few trees. In fact, but for a little fitful post-midnight traffic, there seemed to be hardly any living things in Tucson.

Another intersection, another turn. Back west, this time. Was his subconscious taking him back to the scene of the crime? Telling him to turn himself in now? No. What he wanted was some private place to consider what had happened and what to do about it. He needed to commune with the spirit world. But he didn't have his medicine pouch anymore. And he hadn't packed the rest of his Cheyenne paraphernalia. Not that he actually had to have it, but painting himself, putting on his breechcloth and the headband with the raven feather—it helped him focus on who and what he was. It helped him feel like a Cheyenne shaman, even if the rest of the world thought it was all a bunch of nonsense.

This time the street ended, offering him the choice of north or south. North was wider, brighter, so he went that way even though it would take him back toward Pascua Village. Not a good idea. The police thought he'd killed one of their own. That might lead to a shoot-first-and-ask-later response from any law enforcement agency. In fact, that very concern was why he'd followed Hailey when she ran. And the guy who'd done it, he'd seemed to know exactly what to say and when to say it to deflect the guilt toward Mad Dog. Plus, the guy actually looked Indian. What if Mad Dog's accuser was some well-known local, respected, and believed by the community to be absolutely incapable of killing an officer? And why had the man killed? Mad Dog was going to need contrary theories to that of himself as prime suspect. Right now he didn't have any, and that was why taking time out to commune with the spirits seemed like a good idea.

Then he saw the shop and realized why he'd been driving in circles.

The place was still open. And it would probably stock some of the stuff he needed to make himself feel Indian. He slipped the Mini over into the left lane, made a U-turn, and went back and parked in the vacant lot next to the building. A four-wheel-drive pickup, a Harley, and a battered old Chevy were already parked there.

Hailey stayed in the car when he got out so he didn't worry about leaving the windows down and the doors unlocked, even though this didn't strike him as a great neighborhood. Mostly old motels, some of them the by-the-hour variety. And the business he was going to—well, you wouldn't find what he was looking for in a Circle-K.

Mad Dog pulled the door open. There was a man perusing the magazine racks against one wall. Loud music with a heavy beat boomed from a back room masked by curtains under a sign that said LIVE NUDE GIRLS, 24-7!!! Another guy sat at a counter looking bored.

"What'll it be?" the counter guy asked.

"What have you got in the way of body paint and breech-cloths?" Mad Dog smiled, trying not to look as kinky as the question sounded.

◇◇◇

"Excuse me," Heather said to the stretched blanket that hid the corpse. "Did I hear right? Did you say Mad Dog?"

The man who stood up from behind the blanket was not much taller than Heather. His skin and hair and eyes were very dark and he had cheek bones to die for. He was wearing a uniform that proclaimed him as another Sewa tribal policeman, like the man who'd passed them through the gate.

"Why do you ask?" He stepped around the blanket. He was older than she'd thought at first and there were a couple of bars on his shoulders.

She introduced herself and showed him her Benteen County departmental ID. "My uncle's name is Mad Dog. That's why I wondered."

The man studied her identity card. "He's what, a biker or something?"

"Actually, he's Cheyenne. Me too, partly, though the blood-line gets pretty thin by my generation."

The man nodded, though he didn't look convinced. Heather couldn't blame him. He was so clearly Native American while she looked lily white.

"Your uncle, he was here with you tonight?"

"Ah, no actually. In fact, he's still in Kansas. Or I think he is. But the officer at the gate, he asked us if we'd seen a big bald man and that could be him."

"Describe your uncle for me."

Heather was feeling increasingly uncomfortable. It couldn't be Uncle Mad Dog, not unless he'd gotten her email and hopped in his car first thing this morning and driven straight through. She supposed that was possible. But her uncle was a pacifist and an opponent of capital punishment. There was no way he would have killed anyone.

"Well, he's about six-two, maybe two-fifty. Middle-aged, but fit. He doesn't look Cheyenne. He's fair skinned like me. Oh, and the bald isn't from hair loss. He shaves his head every day."

The man nodded. "He carry a knife?"

"Yeah. Pretty much everybody back home has a pocket knife."

"Describe it."

Heather dug into her Levis and pulled out a small Swiss Army knife. It had an inch-and-a-half blade, a screw driver of similar size, a tooth pick, and a set of tweezers. "Just like this, only his is red, not pink. He gave my sister and me a pair of these when we were still teens because we were always borrowing his."

"How about his chrome-handled switch-blade?" the officer said.

"No," Heather said. "He doesn't own a switchblade. He wouldn't because they're illegal and he wouldn't want to embarrass his brother. My dad's the sheriff."

"Ah," the man nodded, as if that explained why a kid like her was carrying a badge.

"It couldn't be him," Ms. Jardine said.

"And next," the cop said, "I suppose you're going to tell me your uncle doesn't have some kind of huge beast of a dog that follows him around, or drive a red Mini Cooper with Kansas plates?"

Heather's jaw dropped, but she countered the best she could. "Well, he doesn't have a dog. She's a wolf."

◇◇◇

Bits of Mad Dog's house still burned. The fire crew had doused most of them leaving seared patches of lawn that only produced smoke instead of flame.

"Could it have been a gas explosion?" the sheriff asked. What else might cause a house to explode, unless his brother was conducting some sort of strange chemical experiments?

"Nope," the fire chief said. "Checked the propane tank the moment we got here to turn it off so's it wouldn't feed the fire. Thing was already off."

"That's right," English remembered. "Mad Dog was trying to get through the winter without turning on his gas. Said he'd huddle up near his Franklin stove with Hailey and not contribute to our nation's policy of wasting irreplaceable energy resources."

The chief shook his head. Everybody knew Mad Dog was peculiar, but he had a way of making folks feel guilty for not making similar lifestyle choices. "Not many things will cause a house to blow up like that. Mad Dog don't strike me as the type, though I've heard him say he tried most every drug, back in the day. Any chance he might have tried to brew up some methamphetamines?"

The sheriff smiled. Mad Dog had done it all, from grass to LSD to opiates. But that was a long time ago and his brother had turned into one of the cleanest living people you could meet. If peyote was explosive, maybe, since peyote was considered a holy sacrament by some Native American churches. But even that would surprise the sheriff. Mad Dog didn't need substances to get high. Life got him high. Being Cheyenne got him high. Trying to be a shaman got him higher still.

"No," the sheriff said. "Mad Dog might do a lot of crazy things. Turning his house into a meth lab isn't one of them."

The sheriff and the fire chief were wandering about the yard, examining small smoldering clumps that had once been Mad Dog's house or belongings. The sheriff was having a tough go of it because, though it was below freezing again, it was barely so, and the water the fire crew had been spraying was turning into gelatinous mud. Maneuvering his walker across a surface that swallowed its legs instead of supporting them was a problem.

"Hey, Sheriff!" The voice came from over near the road where one of the volunteers had parked his old Dodge pickup. "I think you best come look at this."

The fire chief helped the sheriff extricate the walker from a particularly swampy section and get back onto the hard-packed surface of the driveway, then the two of them headed for the road and the man who'd summoned him.

"What is it?" The moon was nearly full and the sheriff could see that the man was standing next to something dangling from the barbed wire fence that kept Mad Dog's buffalo herd from grazing the freshly sprouted wheat across the way.

"I'm not sure," the man said. "Looks like some big old sawed-off shotgun. There's a webbed sling that appears to have got tangled up in the fence here, like someone in a hurry climbed out of the pasture and dropped this and then couldn't pull it free and didn't feel like hanging around to get it loose."

The sheriff considered the ditch and decided against trying to wade across it. "You got a flashlight you can shine on it?"

The man did and the sheriff recognized it right away. It was a breach-loading M79 grenade launcher. Just like the ones troops were still carrying when he earned a Purple Heart in Southeast Asia.

◇◇◇

A marked Tucson Police Department unit pulled up near the gate while the Sewa officer continued to question Heather and Ms. Jardine. The Tucson officers climbed out of their squad car and the Sewa captain sent one of his men to meet them. Heather picked up just enough of the conversation to understand they were arguing about jurisdiction. When an unmarked car glided in and deposited a couple of suits at the curb, the Sewa captain's face tightened and he stopped his interrogation.

"You two, go and sit on that bench over there." It was back inside the gate. "Don't leave it. I'll be right back."

The women didn't move to obey and he shot them a glare over his shoulder before intercepting the Tucson detectives.

"What do you think?" Ms. Jardine asked.

"I think we've got to be careful here. If we go in there and wait for him and he wins this argument, he just might detain us as material witnesses."

"Yeah. This guy seems to have his heart set on your uncle as the killer." Jardine shook her head. "You really think Mad Dog is here?"

"It sure sounds like it," Heather said. "I mean, this guy knew about Hailey and the Mini Cooper."

"So, what should we do?"

Heather's preference would have been slipping into the shadows and going to look for her uncle, but that wouldn't work. "Why don't you stay here and use my cell. Try Mad Dog. I know it's after two in Kansas, but call my dad next. He needs to know what's going on, especially if we get taken in. He might be able to make some things happen from his end."

"While you do what?"

"I'm going to join that conversation. If somebody takes us into custody, I'd rather be in the hands of your big city pros than a tribal force we don't know anything about. It's too easy for little law enforcement agencies to let the legal niceties slide if that's more convenient. I don't think the Tucson Police Department will do that, especially if you've managed to let Dad know what's happening."

Ms. Jardine agreed. She took Heather's cell phone and started punching numbers. Heather turned toward the street. She got a much angrier glare from the Sewa captain as she pulled her ID and introduced herself to the Tucson detectives.

"Welcome to town, Deputy English," one of them said. "What's your interest in this?"

"We were in the process of establishing that," the Sewa said. "Now, young lady, if you'd just go back over there with your friend and wait for me...."

Heather nodded toward the captain. "This man seems to think my uncle killed his officer. He's wrong about that, but he believes we're withholding evidence instead of cooperating. I thought maybe we should talk to you before he starts the water boarding."

◇◇◇

The sex shop was fresh out of breechcloths, but they had other things Mad Dog could strap on. A selection stood like a row of absurd stalagmites on a nearby display case.

At least they had body paint. Mad Dog decided on the large container of licorice, since he favored a nearly solid black look, except for vanilla lightning bolts. He bought some cherry, as well, to use as tint for the sand painting he wanted to make, and a little blueberry because he liked to mix that and vanilla to highlight the cosmological singularity, even if it wasn't traditional.

Mad Dog would have explained all this to the guy behind the counter, but the man seemed infected by a terminal case of ennui. What marginal interest he managed related to the items that Mad Dog might purchase, not how Mad Dog planned to use them. The guy at the magazine rack, though, moved from the bondage section to spanking—as close as he could get to listen in. Somehow, Mad Dog didn't feel like discussing Cheyenne religious concepts when a man wearing a raincoat on a cloudless evening hovered nearby.

"Anything else?" the counterman muttered.

"There is one thing." Mad Dog could do with some corn pollen, but he was allergic to it. He'd discovered the perfect substitute, however. It was bright and sparkly and he'd first run across the product in a Wichita toy store. "I don't suppose you have any Genuine Official Magic Faerie Dust?"

The counterman's heavy eyelids lifted for the first time. He pulled away, ever so slightly. The guy in the raincoat suddenly decided to browse the most distant magazines, a section labeled FARM ANIMALS.

"No faerie dust?" Mad Dog had picked up on the men's reaction to the "f" word. He flopped a limp wrist in the counterman's direction and asked, "You probably don't have the unrated version of the *Brokeback Mountain* video, either?"

They didn't, and Mad Dog decided to stop amusing himself at their expense. "Just the body paints, then." He paid cash and the counterman took it gingerly.

Mad Dog carried his bag of goods to the front door, where he found he couldn't resist one last barb. "Thank you so much," he said in his best imitation of Truman Capote. "I'll be sure to recommend your wonderful establishment to all my friends."

He minced out onto a deserted sidewalk and closed the door on a pair of horrified expressions. Mad Dog would have laughed, but a sudden flash of headlights reached around the building from the lot where he'd left his Mini. A police cruiser stuck its nose out of the lot and onto the sidewalk and an officer climbed from behind the wheel, cold eyes fixed on Mad Dog as the man reached for his side arm. The officer drew it, but he never managed to point it in Mad Dog's direction. Hailey flew around the corner and took it out of his hand. She passed Mad Dog in an explosion of claws and fur and disappeared around the opposite corner of the building, still carrying the weapon in her teeth.

Mad Dog followed her, as fast as his legs could carry him. It wouldn't take long for the cop to call in back-up. Besides, there was probably a shotgun clamped to the cruiser's dash.

◇◇◇

"What's a grenade launcher doing in Benteen County?" the fire chief muttered, but he couldn't be any more surprised than the sheriff.

His brother, Mad Dog, liked being the county's oddball, the guy who took a contrary stance on every issue. But, here, the worst that usually got him was a sharp retort or a nasty rumor spread behind his back.

"And who'd want to blow up Mad Dog's house?" the chief asked.

Who indeed, the sheriff wondered. Mad Dog had been especially annoying lately. Some out-of-state investors were partnering with the Benteen County Board of Supervisors to push for construction of an ethanol plant in Buffalo Springs. That could result in the biggest job hike in the county since the Gas–Food Mart decided to put on a night shift. And it wasn't just that an ethanol plant would offer new jobs. It could make farming in the county profitable again.

Mad Dog, of course, was against it. He'd been to every local meeting to argue that ethanol production wasn't really environmentally friendly. Sure, it replaced some petroleum in the marketplace, and with a renewable source, but it meant food wasn't being produced. And it took a lot of petroleum products to grow corn. Corn was the most profitable crop to turn into ethanol, so every acre involved in its production would have to be irrigated. Benteen County didn't get enough rainfall to grow it without help. The section of the Ogallala Aquifer under the county had receded from twenty to fifty feet in the last half century. Nobody knew how much farther it might drop. Or whether it might even run out all together. Except Mad Dog, of course, who was certain the ethanol plant would assure the aquifer dried up, after being further polluted by the fertilizers and pesticides that would be used on every acre.

As a result, some folks had been saying pretty nasty things about Mad Dog. Calling him the usual stuff, like pagan, and half-breed. Nutcase had been making the rounds, too. Sheriff English knew a couple of tough old farmers who'd like to duke it out with his brother. But he hadn't heard so much as a whisper about someone throwing a hissyfit and threatening his brother with serious bodily harm. And yet an old grenade launcher had been used on Mad Dog's house, most likely, with the expectation Mad Dog would be home at the time.

Sheriff English tried Mad Dog's cell phone again. Again, it immediately took him to Mad Dog's message box. That meant his brother was either somewhere without service or, as usual, had turned the thing off. Unless it had been somewhere in the ruined house....

The sheriff's daughters might know. One of them was in Tucson. She'd been planning this trip to attend Sandra Day O'Connor's lectures for months. The other, his would-be anthropologist, had called to tell him she was stuck in Lubbock this weekend. He checked his phone and discovered it was almost 2:30. Too late to call Lubbock, and half an hour into Saturday morning in Tucson. He didn't think he should call there, either.

And then he didn't have to, because his cell started chiming in his hand and he could see that Heather was calling him.

"Sheriff. I was afraid I'd wake you." It wasn't Heather's voice.

"Ms. Jardine?" Who else would call from his daughter's phone? "Is something wrong?"

"No. Not yet, anyway. You picked up before the second ring."

"My job is keeping me up late tonight," the sheriff said. Then, "What do you mean not yet?"

"Heather thought you should know. We might end up being held by Tucson or Sewa Tribal Police tonight."

The sheriff almost dropped the phone. "What?"

"There was a murder at the Yaqui Easter ceremonies. An officer got stabbed with a switchblade. It had a name on it, and then there are witnesses who say the killer was a big man with a shaved head who drove off with his huge dog in a Mini Cooper.

"Say," she interrupted herself. "What's going on in Benteen County at this time of night that requires your attention? Where are you?"

The sheriff looked down at the gravel in the driveway beside what had been his brother's house. It glowed. Hunks of smoldering debris turned it golden.

"Looks like I'm at the other end of the yellow brick road Mad Dog drove today," he said. "And I bet you don't have to tell me whose name was on that switchblade."

◇◇◇

The street Mad Dog ran down was lined with industrial buildings and chain-link fence. It offered no place to hide, which made him wonder how Hailey had managed to vanish again. At the first intersection, he zigged north, so he wouldn't be so directly visible from the street where he'd left the sex shop and the disarmed cop. That officer was going to be pissed. He'd get himself another gun and some back-up and come looking for Mad Dog all too soon.

This block proved no more conducive to hiding than the last. Mad Dog zagged at the next intersection, heading west, away from the street with the lights and farther into a dilapidated industrial zone.

Finally, midway down the block, he came on what had once been a house. Its front yard was paved for parking, now, but there were at least some shadowy spots against its cracked plaster walls where scraggly oleanders offered partial concealment. He ducked behind one with a few pale blossoms. He could see through the bush, which wasn't reassuring, but he needed a moment to consider where to go, and how, and what he might do when he got there.

It seemed likely that he would soon be going to jail. Or, accompanying someone from the coroner's office if they decided to shoot first, next time, before the wonder wolf could disarm them again and give him another chance to flee.

One block to the south, a car drove slowly west. Not just any car, judging from the bright spotlights it used to peer into lots filled with dirt and weeds and junked machinery behind razor-wire topped chain link. He could hear tires coming along this street, too. Reinforcements? If not now, soon.

He reached into his bag of merchandise, found the body paint, and swabbed his head, face, and hands with licorice. Rolled his sleeves down, too, though there wasn't much he could do about the plaid shirt he wore. Like camouflage, it contained a variety of colors and patterns. Unfortunately, none of them remotely resembled anything found in nature.

He ducked as the second car arrived. Spotlights turned his hiding place as bright as the surface of the sun. Mad Dog tried to make himself as undetectable as Hailey had become. The bright red patches of his shirt seemed to glow, reflecting the luminosity of that police spotlight.

The police car slowed. Stopped. The light pinned him against the wall.

Invisible, invisible, invisible, Mad Dog told himself. The blinding light moved on. The police car moved with it. And Hailey stood on the other side of the oleanders, whining with impatience and the clear desire that he follow her.

Well, hell. If she'd just succeeded in making them both undetectable to those cops, he'd follow her anywhere she wanted.

◇◇◇

"Water boarding." The detective laughed. "Not likely from Captain Matus, here. The Sewa live on a desert reservation. They know water is too rare to waste torturing prisoners. I figure he's more likely to peel off your fingernails and, if that doesn't work, skin you alive."

From the way Matus glared at Heather, she wasn't sure the man was kidding. "Either way," she said, "I've got nothing to confess. Not for myself or on behalf of my uncle. And what's Matus' authority here? Why Sewa tribal police instead of Yaqui?"

"Yaquis have a real small force they use mostly at their casino," the detective said. "Guess they farmed this out."

"Enough of this bull," Matus interrupted. "That was my officer who took a knife in the chest. Our cousins, the Yaqui Nation, hired us to provide security for this ceremony and I've got a right to question these witnesses."

The detective shook his head. "You got no legal jurisdiction here, Matus. This isn't your Rez. This may be a Yaqui community, but it's inside the City of Tucson."

The second detective held his hands up, palms open, like he was using sign language to indicate peaceful intent. "I don't see why Captain Matus can't join us for any questioning to be done."

Matus smirked in Heather's direction, like maybe he was getting more than he'd expected. "I can live with that," he said.

"So can I," Heather said, after glancing Ms. Jardine's way and getting a nod that indicated her dad was in the loop. "I don't mean any insult to the Captain or his police force, but he was coming on pretty strong. I didn't want to take a chance that we might disappear into some legal limbo. With the Tucson Police Department involved, and with the Sheriff of Benteen County, Kansas having been informed, that's no longer a concern for me."

Matus pounced on that. "That's your father she has on the phone? Let me talk to him."

Heather couldn't think of why not. She waved Ms. Jardine over and the woman gave the captain Heather's cell.

"This is Captain Matus of the Sewa Tribal Police. Who're you?"

He paused while Englishman answered.

"I assume you're aware of what's happened here tonight. Have you been told about the description witnesses gave of the killer? Is your brother in Kansas, Sheriff English?"

"Is he?" Heather asked. Jardine shook her head.

"His house, you say? Tonight? That's remarkable. So, if I call your office they can confirm all this?"

"What about Mad Dog's house?" Heather whispered.

"Someone blew it up."

Matus nearly blew up, too. "You're kidding me. You're telling me your office isn't staffed? All right, I'll give you fifteen minutes to get there. Then expect an official call on the number listed for your agency. And expect us to call some other Kansas agencies to find out if you're for real. And why your office isn't open twenty-four hours a day. Until we can confirm who you are, Ms. English and Ms. Jardine will remain in custody."

"Ours," the Tucson detective said. "Not his. And just so we can ask you a few more questions. We need help from you ladies to get us up to speed on this."

The women nodded.

"I see," Matus concluded. He folded the phone shut and turned to the Tucson detectives. "I'd like to introduce you gentlemen to Deputy Heather English. She works for her daddy. As, I suspect, all of her brothers do, if she has any, and they're probably all named Daryll."

Heather blushed. Matus had hit too close with his insult. Her adopted sister was also named Heather. That had caused lots of confusion and a few laughs over the years. Tonight, it didn't seem even faintly amusing.

◇◇◇

As far as Mad Dog could tell, the search hadn't spread to the east side of Oracle Road yet. So far, following Hailey had kept him out of custody, if not out of trouble. Not that the stabbing had been her fault.

They were in a little motor court on a dark street a couple of blocks northeast of the sex shop. Or what had been a motor court half a century ago. Now it was just a cluster of concrete block apart-ments with rusty evaporative coolers in the windows. The yard down the middle of the complex didn't grow grass anymore, just sand, dirt, weeds, and the occasional rock. The whole place was badly in need of fix-up and fresh paint, except where taggers had recently marked it with graffiti. Mad Dog couldn't figure out why Hailey had brought him to these apartments, even if he needed a place to hole up and the sign out front said they had units for rent. Then he noticed a pay phone at the rear of the complex on a wall beside a door labeled LAUNDRY/STORAGE. With his cell phone still in the Mini Cooper, the pay phone would come in handy. He turned to look at Hailey and shake his head in wonder. Once again, she was gone. He shook his head anyway, and didn't worry about her. She'd come back when she was ready.

As he headed for the phone, someone backed out of the laundry room. It was a tall, bulked up man with thick shoulders and long hair and tattoos crawling out from under ragged shirt sleeves. Not someone Mad Dog wanted to meet in a dark alley. Or here, even if the guy was toting a basket of clean clothes. The man turned and noticed Mad Dog and his eyes got wide. He dropped his laundry and sprinted to the third apartment down, frantically grabbing for keys. He ducked inside and slammed the door behind him. Mad Dog heard him throw the bolt. Apparently, one resident of the apartment complex didn't want to meet someone slathered in licorice body paint in the dark either.

The guy didn't re-emerge with a gun or start calling for help, so Mad Dog went to the phone and dug some change out of his pocket. As usual, there was nothing but a handful of pennies. Damn, he thought, and then noticed the shiny spots atop the big guy's spilled laundry. He bent and checked and, sure enough, they were quarters. Mad Dog collected all of them he could find. He picked up the laundry and put it back in the basket, too, though after contacting bare earth, it would need to be washed again. He placed a twenty dollar bill on top of the stack and weighted it down with a convenient rock.

There wasn't much doubt about who he should call. What could either of the Heathers do for him? What could anyone do for him? Except....

"Sheriff English," his brother answered, surprisingly alert for this godforsaken hour.

"Hey, bro," Mad Dog said. "You'll never guess what's happened to me tonight."

"Wanna bet? My daughter and Ms. Jardine are being held as witnesses right now, and I'm on my way to the courthouse to be there to answer a call from a very angry policeman so I can prove I'm the sheriff. All because you're supposed to have stabbed another policeman to death less than an hour ago."

"Oh," Mad Dog said. Since his brother already knew, it would save a lot of time. Still, he felt a little let down that he couldn't be the first to pass along the news. "Well, I didn't do it."

"Never thought you did," Englishman said. "But why'd you run? My advice is to give yourself up. Right now!"

"I know I should do that, Englishman, but it doesn't feel real safe. And I wouldn't have run in the first place if Hailey wasn't leading the way."

That caused Englishman to pause. Mad Dog knew his brother didn't buy into the whole Cheyenne Shamanism thing the way Mad Dog had, even if they shared the same bloodline. But Englishman didn't completely discount it, either, and no one who knew her doubted Hailey had an amazing knack for being in the right place at the right time. Back in Benteen County, even folks who were scared she might kill their sheep and calves tended to call her the Wonder Wolf.

"Can I get back to you at this number?" Englishman asked. "I know somebody in Tucson who might help, but I'm going to have to do some searching to find a phone number. And, I'll be talking to law enforcement down there. Maybe I can arrange a safe way for you to surrender."

"I'll feel a lot better about doing that after they've got the real killer. I know who that is, by the way."

"You do? Why didn't you say so?"

"He's going to be real easy to find," Mad Dog continued. "Just go to my house and…."

"You don't have a house anymore, Mad Dog," Englishman interrupted. "Somebody put a rocket-propelled grenade through your window tonight. There's not much left."

Mad Dog's jaw dropped. His house? Their mother's mementos, his books, irreplaceable letters, his Cheyenne paraphernalia—all gone?

"But your buffalo herd is all right. And the outbuildings are still there, though some are a little singed."

"Damn!" Mad Dog said. "Then maybe he's won."

"Who? The killer? Who are you talking about?"

"Yeah, the killer—Fig Zit."

"Who?"

"Fig, like the fruit. And Zit like a pimple," Mad Dog said.

"That's a stupid name," Englishman said.

Mad Dog found that a bit unkind, considering his own name. "It's not stupid," he said, "not if you're a level seventy Coalition vampire wizard."

◇◇◇

A level thirty-one Coalition bloodknight warrior was killing Mrs. Kraus for the fourth time in a row when the phone rang. If that damn Coalition bastard had let her finish even one quest in the last half hour, she might not have answered it. She wasn't supposed to be in the office. Her shift didn't start until eight and the current board of supervisors didn't want her putting in any overtime. She glanced at the clock. It was getting toward three in the morning. She couldn't imagine who might call at this time.

It was those damn night sweats, again. And the fact that she didn't seem to need hardly any sleep anymore. She was always tired, but the only time she felt sleepy these days was when it wasn't bed time. So, she'd gotten up and gone to the bathroom and debated going back to bed and lying there and willing herself to sleep. But that never worked. She turned on the TV and couldn't find anything remotely interesting. And that settled it. She'd raised her League human warrior to level twenty-three last night, playing War of Worldcraft on the office computer after the courthouse cleared out. So, here she was, being chased around Drylands by the bloodknight who was probably just some pubescent computer geek who lived in a time zone like Alaska or Hawaii.

"Well damn," she said, as the bloodknight stole all but the last of her health with a sweep of his double-bladed ax. She felt like pulling out her Glock and blowing up both bloodknight and the computer monitor, but she grabbed the phone instead, just before its fourth ring. It could be a real emergency.

"Benteen County Sheriff's Office," she said.

"I didn't think this office was supposed to be open," a male voice said.

"Then why'd you call?" Mrs. Kraus had one of those voices that had gone beyond whiskey and cigarettes to pure white lightning and locoweed. Her tones were about as mellow as barbed wire scraped across a blackboard.

"Is Sheriff English there?"

Mrs. Kraus turned back to her computer screen. Sure enough, her warrior was dead and the bloodknight was dancing on her corpse. "Screw you," she muttered to the bloodknight.

"What's that? What did you say?" The guy on the phone had gone from testy to belligerent.

"I wasn't speaking to you," Mrs. Kraus said. "I'm a little busy here. You want Sheriff English? He don't stay in this office around the clock. It's damn near three a.m."

"The sheriff guaranteed me he'd be in his office to answer this phone by…well, less than five minutes from now."

She didn't believe him. Englishman would be home in bed, or dealing with his own insomnia in his own way. He shared her problem, what with the pain he was in from that gunshot wound and the loss he still felt over watching his wife's losing battle with cancer. And, since his daughters had gone off to college, it had to be damn lonely in the sheriff's house these days.

"Then maybe you should call back," Mrs. Kraus said. "Until you do, you have yourself a real nice morning, you hear?"

"This is Captain…." She didn't catch the rest. She wasn't much interested in dealing with some wacko with an attitude when she wasn't getting paid for it. Besides, surely that bloodknight would tire of killing her over and over before long. And she knew where she could maybe get at a treasure chest over the other side of that camp of life-sucking dust bunnies. She reached for the mouse to begin the process of resurrecting her corpse when the door flew open and Englishman came gimping in on his walker.

"Mrs. Kraus," he said. "What are you doing here?"

She was in a foul mood, and embarrassed at getting caught. "I'm playing a computer game," she said, "if it's any of your business. Which, since this is the sheriff's department's computer in your office, I suppose it is."

"I thought you…." That's all he managed when the phone rang again. She had a pretty good idea what he would have said, though. She mostly refused to do computers. Didn't have one of her own, nor a cell phone. Hell, she still changed the channels on her TV by hand. People thought of her as a technophobe, and she supposed she was. But boredom and curiosity had lured her into this massive-multiplayer-online-role-playing game Mad Dog had gotten so involved with. And, while it drove her nuts lots of the time, she had to admit she was hooked. Hard to claim otherwise when she'd come down to the office to play it at this ungodly hour.

"Sheriff English," he said into the phone. And after a moment, "That would be my office manager, Mrs. Kraus. And if she was rude to you, I don't doubt you deserved it."

Mrs. Kraus smiled and her mood improved. Especially when it occurred to her she might be able to lure that bloodknight into getting ambushed by a host of dust bunnies.

◇◇◇

Captain Matus was exasperated. "What do you mean you won't hold these women?"

They were an hour into Saturday morning and he'd been up since before the previous dawn. Worse, this was the first time he'd lost an officer in the line of duty. Matus wanted this Mad Dog guy now.

"I mean we're *not* going to hold them," said the Tucson detective, the one with the dandruff all over his sports coat.

Matus sighed. "Explain it to me."

"Okay." The detective rubbed a hand through the stubble of his crew cut, adding to the drifts of flakes covering his shoulders. "This Deputy English, she's attending law school at Kansas University. She gets invited to a symposium at the University of Arizona presented by Sandra Day O'Connor—who, from what we're told, might personally come down to file a writ of habeas corpus if we take these ladies in. Deputy English's story holds water. The law student who was her host at the seminar confirmed it. Says the woman Ms. English is staying with suggested they visit these Easter ceremonies. Says the girl was so blown away by what she saw that she tried to call her uncle. Never got him, but left an email message.

"Now we've talked to her dad. We know he really is a sheriff, even if it's just of some podunk county in the middle of nowhere. And we know your suspect's house was destroyed by a grenade launcher tonight. The man's not there and his car is gone, so he could be here in Tucson. Probably is, since your witnesses' descriptions match the ones these ladies and the sheriff gave us.

"But then we run into a problem. You've lost the guy who identified this Mad Dog as the killer. The rest of your witnesses saw something happen and the knife has your suspect's name on it. But the only guy who actually saw your officer getting stabbed has disappeared."

"He's some big deal Sioux medicine man we weren't expecting," Matus said. "Lots of people in our community have heard of him, though. We've got his home address as well as the hotel room where he's staying. He's for real."

"But, right now, you don't know where he is. And these ladies and your suspect's brother all say Mad Dog is a pacifist who would never own a switchblade, let alone harm anyone—except to prevent them from harming someone else. Even then, they say, he'd probably just try to talk them out of it."

"Of course they'd say that." Matus banged a fist on the table. "They're trying to protect him."

"Could be, but we've already got word this Sheriff English has a reputation for honesty," the younger Tucson detective said. "His daughter does too. This other lady seems like a bit of a loon, but she checks out as a local business woman. We don't think there's more to get out of either of them. Maybe if you had that missing witness and he tied them in somehow…."

"He's probably consulting with some Yaqui *Maestros*," Matus said. "We'll turn him up soon."

"Good," Dandruff said. "Meanwhile, there's no reason to detain these ladies any longer."

Matus opened his mouth for another protest but the detectives were on their feet and going through the door to the room where the women waited.

"You're both free to go," Dandruff told them, "as long as you head straight home, Ms. Jardine. You're to continue staying with her, Ms. English. And don't leave town before we tell you it's okay."

"Fine," Heather said.

"But her uncle may try to contact them," Matus whispered to Dandruff.

"Gee," Dandruff said, "I wish that had occurred to me."

"We expect to have Mr. Mad Dog in custody before dawn," Dandruff's partner said. "See if you can't match that with his accuser."

"Come on," Dandruff told the women. "Let me arrange for an escort."

"That's not necessary," Heather said.

The officer shrugged and flakes fell again, but Matus was relieved by his response. "Actually, it is."

◇◇◇

He didn't look Sioux anymore. Now he looked like someone whose family had come from the eastern Mediterranean. The wig with the braids, the beaded headband, and all his silver jewelry had been stuffed in a greasy bag under a partially eaten burger and fries and deposited in a foul-smelling dumpster behind a fast food restaurant near the sprawling university. The moccasins he'd been wearing and the IDs he'd been carrying had accompanied them. After donning a pair of loafers and a sports coat, and smoothing his own close-cropped hair, he looked nothing like the Indian Medicine Man he'd been earlier in the evening.

Walking out the back exit to Pasqua Village had been simple in the midst of all that confusion. No one had seen him climb into his rental car and drive away. Just in case, though, he'd swapped it for the backup he'd left on a residential street several neighborhoods closer to the university, and several levels up the income ladder. He didn't bother dusting his prints from the car he abandoned. He didn't have fingerprints anymore. And he'd borrowed some items from the rooms of several hotels to confuse any DNA trail. He was good at this. He was a professional and he took pride in his work. Pleasure, too.

He was on Kino Boulevard, heading for the airport when his cell rang. It surprised him. He'd just activated this one. No one should know its number yet. Not even his client for tonight's job. That was how you protected yourself. You left no trail. If the money he was owed didn't appear in his numbered account in that Caribbean bank when it should, he was the one who would reestablish contact.

He answered without saying anything. A voice he'd come to recognize, deep and heavy with authority, said, "Nice job at Pasqua. But Mad Dog got away."

How had the man gotten his new number? This was a security breach he couldn't live with. Or, more precisely, that this client couldn't be allowed to live with. But he couldn't fix that now. For the moment, all he could do was decide how to minimize this new risk.

"You didn't instruct me to see that he was caught or captured. Only to make him appear to be the cold-blooded killer of that officer during the ceremony."

The voice on the phone chuckled. "Don't worry. I'm not faulting my assassin. The final payment for this project has already been transferred to the account you specified. If there's fault here, it's mine for not anticipating the possibility that Mad Dog would try to escape. It's out of character for him. Unusual in any innocent man."

"Which begs the question of why you've contacted me," the professional said, and thought, *to say nothing of how.*

"I'd like to arrange a new contract. There's someone in Tucson Mad Dog may try to get in touch with who might help him clear himself. I'd like you to convince that person he's dangerous. And then I'd like you to see to it that Mad Dog isn't taken alive. Shall we say double your original fee? And double that if you can manage to wrap this up before noon today."

The man who had penetrated his security would have to be eliminated, but it was going to take time to determine what had gone wrong and what changes of procedure he needed to make. And finding a client who could pierce his defenses might not be easy, or cheap. The extra money would help.

"Half now? The rest on completion?"

"The moment you agree I'll make the first transfer."

"Do it," the professional said, turning off Kino to head back into town. "Then tell me who you want convinced and just how thoroughly."

"How, I'll leave to your imagination. It shouldn't be difficult for a man of your skills—one who has demonstrated them so recently."

"Who and where?"

He didn't have to write down the information his troublesome client supplied. He had a perfect memory—total recall. That was excellent, because he could remember every detail of the suffering of every victim he'd ever killed. And enjoy them over and over again at his leisure.

◇◇◇

English maneuvered his walker over behind Mrs. Kraus' chair. "Are you playing War of Worldcraft?" he asked.

"Don't you go making fun of me," she said. "Ain't nothing worth watching on television anymore, 'specially this time of morning. I realize this is the county's computer, but I ain't hurting it none and besides, I'm on my own time and…."

"Whoa," Englishman said. "I'm not accusing you of anything. I'm just wondering if you and Mad Dog have been playing the same game."

Mrs. Kraus took a deep breath. She hadn't realized how guilty she felt about what she was doing. It was county property and she didn't have permission to be here or to use it. And she was using electricity. But the county was still a couple of months behind on the paychecks they owed her. That had made her late-night adventures in the courthouse seem like reasonable interest on what she was owed, until her boss caught her in the act.

"Yes," she said. "This is War of Worldcraft."

"What Mad Dog plays?" the sheriff continued.

"Yes sir, this is the copy he gave you once he commenced to get interested. Only you never tried it. Besides, I pay the monthly access fees myself. They bill it to my credit card and…."

"No, really, Mrs. Kraus. I don't care what you do down here with the computer on your own time. It's just…Mad Dog said some strange things to me when he called. He seemed to think he could identify the man who killed that officer in Arizona tonight. Or, not the man exactly, the character—somebody who's been causing havoc for him whenever he plays this game. I don't suppose you've ever run into a, what was it, a vampire wizard, I think? A real powerful character named Fig Zit?"

"That'd probably be a seventy," Mrs. Kraus said. "I'm too lowly for a seventy to bother with. I may not even be playing on the same server as Mad Dog. Still, I don't see how some character from this silly game could have anything to do with a real-life murder."

"Mad Dog said, once he thought on it, that this guy who knifed a cop to death looked like the Fig Zit character from the game. It's not much to go on, but we're half a country away from Mad Dog and Heather, and it's the wee hours of the morning when the little I can do from here gets even smaller. But maybe we could track down this Fig Zit."

Mrs. Kraus shook her head. "Not gonna be that easy. There's millions of players, and lots of security on internet programs like this. We got to know Mad Dog's log-in and his password. He give that to you?"

"No," the sheriff admitted. "He didn't. He hung up on me after I told him his house was destroyed."

Mrs. Kraus only knew the little she'd overheard during his phone call, so she made him stop and give her the details, as well as an outline of Mad Dog's adventures in Arizona.

"So he's without his cell phone? You can't call him back?"

The sheriff nodded.

"Well, that don't mean we can't discover his log-in. Might take us a few tries, but I'd bet Mad Dog ain't been too subtle." She turned back to the computer and hit the button that took her out of the game and to the log-in screen. She typed in "maddog," explaining, "You can't use spaces." For the password, she typed "hailey." The log-in failed and Mrs. Kraus changed the password to "haileymarie," the wolf's more formal name. It failed again.

"I'm open to suggestions," she said. "Cheyenne, maybe, or he might use the Cheyenne's name for themselves. You remember what that is?"

"Tsistsistas," Englishman said.

Mrs. Kraus asked him how to spell it.

"No," Englishman said. "That would be too obvious to anyone who knows him. Hailey's name probably was, too."

"What, then?"

"Try Pam, or Pam Epperson."

"That girl he's involved with? She gave him this game, didn't she? I remember now. It sure never seemed like something he'd buy for himself."

Pam Epperson was way too young for Mad Dog, but they'd developed a surprisingly stable relationship, and she'd breathed some youth back into the sheriff's brother.

Englishman smiled. "He said she didn't want him having any adventures without her unless they were the virtual kind."

Mrs. Kraus harrumphed—something between disapproval and jealousy—but she entered the girl's name and the screen changed. "Log-in successful," it said. "Loading characters."

There was only one character—Madwulf, a level fifty-two League human shaman.

"If I'd been betting," Mrs. Kraus said, "I'd've put money on him being a shaman. But I sure would've bet against him rising this high so fast."

"Fifty-two, that's good?"

"More'n double me, and it gets harder each level you climb."

"Can we get in the game? Can we look for this Fig Zit?"

"Oh sure. That's easy now. " Mrs. Kraus pushed a couple of buttons and a few moments later a bald, robed figure that looked a little like Mad Dog stood beneath an angelic shape amidst a collection of tombstones on a screen that had gone black and white.

"Funny," Mrs. Kraus said. "He left his character dead. I always heal mine and find an inn to hole up in 'cause then you advance faster the next time you play."

"You can heal when you're dead?" Englishman obviously didn't have much experience with computer games where death was only a temporary inconvenience.

"Just got to find his body," Mrs. Kraus said, maneuvering Madwulf around a tree and through a gate.

"What's that, then?" the sheriff asked, pointing at the figure on the screen.

"His spirit. We'll put some color in his cheeks when we resurrect him."

"How do you do that?" Englishman had been a cop too long not to ask for explanations of everything he didn't understand. She liked that about him.

"Just get near his body and the program will give us the option. See that little circle up in the corner? That's a map. That tombstone, that's his body. The arrow, that's his spirit. Shows us which way we're heading and which way we need to go, though sometimes the terrain doesn't cooperate."

A huge chasm opened directly in their path but Mrs. Kraus maneuvered neatly around it.

"This is a little more elaborate than Pong." That was probably the last computer game the sheriff had played. Likely, the only one.

The land fell away below them into rolling hills with, here and there, trees big enough to put sequoias to shame. Waterfalls cascaded from the larger ones.

"Here he is." A little box appeared on the screen. "Resurrect," it said. Not far beyond, a body lay sprawled on lush grass.

Mrs. Kraus hit the button and the world turned more magical as color flooded the moonlit sward and birds and butterflies swooped among the trees. Mrs. Kraus clicked on another button and a container opened that held all sorts of unlikely objects. She picked the peanutberry jam sandwich and Madwulf sat in the grass and began eating. "Up in the left corner," she said. "That's his health and his spell casting ability. See how both are getting stronger as he eats? We'll have him going in a...."

"You can't be here," a voice roared at them. It sounded like it should come from a burning bush. Or maybe James Earl Jones trying to mimic Orson Welles. "How'd you get to a computer? You should be on the run."

A figure appeared out of nowhere. Materializing, as if Scotty had just beamed him down from the Starship Enterprise. He was dark and trim with black, braided hair held out of his face by a beaded band just over his eyebrows.

"Lordy," Mrs. Kraus said. She punched the keyboard like mad and a little message appeared in a balloon over Madwulf's head.

"What do you want with me, Fig Zit?"

"What do I want with you?" the voice boomed. "I want you dead, Mad Dog. Just like that officer in Pascua Village. Just like this."

A lightning bolt pierced the sky and all the little lines for Madwulf's health and spell casting emptied. He pitched forward onto the grass, exactly as he had been when they found him. The voice laughed maniacally.

"Damn!" Englishman said. "I think we just found the thing that crazy brother of mine thinks is the killer."

◇◇◇

Sergeant Parker's hand grabbed her SIG-Sauer instead of the phone when it rang. And didn't let go as her other hand reached for the alarm clock and turned it so she could see the face—1:37. Jesus! She'd been asleep maybe an hour. She finally snatched the phone as it began its third ring, but she kept the SIG in her shooting hand. She felt like blowing away whoever was calling, but bullets didn't travel down phone lines very well.

"Parker," she said, crisp and formal and alert. In every way, contrary to how she felt.

"Hope I didn't wake you," a voice she didn't quite recognize murmured in her ear.

"Wake me? Who sleeps at one-thirty in the morning?" The man at the other end of the phone line didn't laugh, but then she hadn't meant it as a joke. "What can I do for you?"

"I'm not sure, Sergeant."

She had it now—Deputy Chief Dempsey. She didn't like him much because he had a thing about working with women who had authority of their own and exercised it.

"Bomb?" she asked. It was a logical question. She was the top explosives expert in Tucson law enforcement.

He surprised her. "No. Homicide. Of a Sewa officer at Pasqua Village's Easter ceremonies about midnight. Suspect got away from tribal police, then gave the slip to one of our patrolmen at a neighborhood sex shop maybe half an hour later."

She couldn't figure out what this had to do with her, but she didn't give him the satisfaction of asking.

"We've had roundabout contact with the suspect, since. Some people think he might be willing to give himself up to you."

Parker tried to think who it could be. The only person who came to mind was a former date she'd never seen again after proving she wasn't someone you tried to get rough with. But that guy had taken a job with a security firm in Iraq where rough was how everybody played.

"Why?" She was a woman of few words. Especially at this time of the morning.

"He knows you. Trusts you. His brother thinks he can persuade the man to surrender to you."

"Am I supposed to guess who you're talking about, Chief, or are you going to tell me?"

Dempsey chuckled. He'd gotten to her, which was what he'd been trying to do from the beginning of the conversation. In his mind, he'd just bested her and proved women didn't belong in his department.

"Remember your retirement after that mishap at Glenn and Wilson?"

Years ago, a woman had died at the corner of Glenn and Wilson. Parker had made a mistake, and then she'd made another by trying to run away from it. She'd run all the way to a rural Kansas county where she'd never have to deal with bombs and choices that could kill innocent citizens again. Except life didn't necessarily play out that way. Her second experience with a bomb helped her heal from the first, and eventually brought her back to Tucson. And it made her determined to understand everything there was to know about explosives and how to keep them from going boom. That second chance had been five years ago. But she knew the suspect's name now. It came to her just as fast as the flood of memories caused by mention of that north-central Tucson intersection.

"Harvey Edward Mad Dog," she said.

"Ah." She could hear the smile in Dempsey's voice. "So you *do* know our killer."

"I know Mad Dog. Sheriff English's brother may be about the oddest man I've ever met, but he's also about the gentlest. If he's the best suspect you've come up with, your case is in a world of hurt."

You couldn't hear jaws drop over the telephone. She just hoped Mad Dog hadn't changed in the years since she'd seen him last—gone psycho or something. She liked it when the Bomb Broad managed to put Assistant Chief Dempsey back under his rock.

◇◇◇

It wasn't the shock of losing his home. It wasn't even the incineration of his computer—his only link to the killer he'd met in War of Worldcraft—that caused Mad Dog to hang up on his brother. It was a marked TPD car slowly creeping past the front of the apartments.

He was many blocks from there, now. South, toward downtown, though not for any special reason. Hailey hadn't put in an appearance and he thought she would if he were going the wrong way.

He didn't have much of a plan. Just finding another phone, isolated enough for a Cheyenne shaman in war paint to use without arousing undue interest. Any interest, actually, since his licorice head and hands were going to be a problem for anyone he met.

The black paint made good camouflage as he followed a succession of back streets and dusty alleys. And more than one patrol car had cruised by, uncomfortably close, but without spotting him. He wasn't ready to wash the stuff off yet.

Mad Dog was still at a loss to explain what had happened to him on this strange night. The only thing that made sense to him was that Fig Zit really was a vampire wizard, or some real-world equivalent—a being who could reach into the game, or out of it, and touch him anywhere. That wasn't comforting, but, since Pascua, Fig Zit hadn't caused him more problems. Of course, Mad Dog had enough already.

He was in a confusing area where the streets were all numbered, both north/south and east/west. Avenues went toward Mexico and Canada. Streets toward the coasts. Not that he knew where he was going except in the direction of the three unimpressive skyscrapers that marked what must be downtown. He'd chosen that direction only because he thought he could find another pay phone in the business district.

This was a mixed residential area. And not a high-dollar one, either. Tired old adobes sat among faded brick and dry-rotted wood homes, with here and there the odd bit of gentrification.

A few dogs announced his passing, though no one paid enough attention to investigate. He glanced at his watch—3:57 Kansas time, 1:57 here. No great surprise if homeowners ignored their animals' warnings.

A pair of huge Rottweilers and a neighboring Pit Bull were making so much noise that he rounded a corner into a little cluster of late-night drinkers without noticing them. When he did, he was practically in the middle of a group of dusky figures sipping from tall cans as they sat under trees, on the fenders of a pair of shiny old Chevys, and on the low wall that separated a grassless front yard from the broken sidewalk. He might not have noticed them at all if one of the men hadn't flipped a glowing cigarette into the street. The situation was short on suitable options. Turn and run, continue forward and try to bluff his way past, or ask if they could spare him a beer.

"Hi," Mad Dog said, nodding toward one side of the sidewalk, then the other. No one responded, though all of them stopped talking and turned to watch him.

"Nice night," Mad Dog said, approaching the last of them.

"Hey, mofo," a voice said, thick with drink and threat and Black street-drawl. "What minstrel show you escape from?"

Shit, Mad Dog thought. Maybe Fig Zit had arranged more trouble for him after all.

◇◇◇

"Can we talk to Fig Zit the way he talks to us?" the sheriff asked.

Fig Zit had blasted Madwulf with lightning and fire three straight times. The last time, he'd gotten creative and added some flaming snowballs.

Mrs. Kraus shook her head. "Not without special add-on software. Maybe even hardware, stuff I don't know about."

The sheriff was disappointed. "So the only way we can communicate with him is hope he doesn't kill us before you finish typing your message."

"Well," Mrs. Kraus admitted, "I didn't think of it, but we don't have to resurrect Madwulf right there in plain sight. We can hunt around some and maybe find a hidey hole. Has to be close, though, but I just might get off something before he fries us again."

The sheriff rubbed his chin in thought. "So our message has to be short. Something that grabs his attention and makes him *want* to talk to us."

"Interrogating him, that'd be good. But I don't see how we're going to learn anything useful. It's not like you can hustle him back into one of our cells. He can just blast us or disappear anytime he wants."

"We'll never know unless we try. Log in again, Mrs. Kraus."

They hunted around the spot where Madwulf's body lay at the edge of a meadow. One of the great waterfall trees was just behind them and they hid in the mist near its trunk.

"This might work, "Mrs. Kraus said. "Though it's awful close to that covey of forest sprites. If we're too close, they'll pounce on us as quick as Fig Zit. One, we might fight off. More'n that'll kill us. Slower, but just as sure."

"Try it."

Madwulf materialized from the ether, resurrected yet again. A pair of forest sprites turned and began coming his way.

"What do you want me to say?" Mrs. Kraus asked.

"Tell him we know who he is."

As Mrs. Kraus finished the message the forest sprites were on them. Beautiful, scantily-clad human-like females that attacked with slashing teeth and extended claws. Madwulf began defending himself but his health was fading fast. And then the forest sprites melted into small puddles of glowing viscera and Fig Zit loomed over them.

"You know who I am? And who would that be?"

"What do I tell him now?" Mrs. Kraus asked.

That, the sheriff thought, was an excellent question.

◇◇◇

The professional knew modern police had access to remarkable computer programs, even in the field. Fortunately, they also employed lots of technophobes. All he needed to keep track of what police forces were doing was a radio that monitored the right frequencies. It was just another tool of his trade.

That was how the professional learned about the sex shop Mad Dog had visited. Why he knew about the body paint his target had purchased. The professional had all that information well before he arrived at the near west-side address his client had supplied. Long enough in advance to find a Wal-Mart, one that wasn't open and thus wouldn't record a sale or remember a purchaser.

Before starting this job, he'd researched Mad Dog. Mad Dog hadn't been his target then, but the professional was supposed to make certain Mad Dog appeared to be the killer. That meant knowing enough to understand how the would-be Cheyenne was likely to behave. The professional had heard about Mad Dog's annual vision quests in the park across from the Benteen County courthouse. He only needed black and white paint to mimic Mad Dog's preferred design.

When the professional needed last minute supplies, he liked to shop at Wal-Mart. They carried everything, even body paint, or what could be used for the purpose, if you knew where to look. And it didn't matter that they weren't open when he made his shopping runs. Wal-Marts were the same everywhere, including their security arrangements. He went in, fast and quiet and easy, and took what he needed.

The house he was looking for was in the Menlo Park area. Tucson had big plans for downtown renovation and downtown was just east, across the freeway. The neighborhood seemed to be upgrading. Not that some of the houses hadn't already been desirable. This target lived in one of those—a single-story brick with an odd configuration that must have seemed ultra-modern when it was built shortly after World War II.

He began with a drive-by surveillance. The iron fence with its spear-like tips could be a problem. So could the fact that it appeared the homeowner was up and about. A light went on in a window as he cruised past. She was at home, at least. He wouldn't have to go hunting for her.

He left his car a couple of blocks away, near the foot of a small volcanic peak on which the mandatory letter "A" was outlined. Tucson was, after all, home to the University of Arizona.

He stripped down and applied the paint. Black everywhere, but for bright and jagged lightning bolts on his arms and legs and cheeks. Mad Dog wore homemade breechcloths these days, but he'd been known to make do with Speedos when he first got started. The professional thought black briefs would do. And then there was the final touch. The hatchet he'd liberated from Wal-Mart's hardware department. Eventually, an inventory would show the Tucson store was missing some merchandise. But they'd never know he'd broken in. Shoplifters, or disloyal employees, would get the blame.

Wal-Mart had shoes for every purpose. Most of his purposes required good traction and low visibility, especially at night. Matching the black body paint wasn't a problem.

The light he'd seen was out by the time he got back to the house. Another was on in a different room. He could see a shadow moving around in there. He thought she might be up and getting ready to leave. He used the limb of a shade tree to go over the spiked metal wall and made short work of the locks on the back door. Having no pockets, he put the picks in his mouth and reviewed his preparations.

He didn't have a headband or a feather. Too little time to find and redesign a headdress from the toy department, and it wasn't something his victim was likely to notice.

He hadn't shaved his head, either. A black swim cap would do nicely. As he slipped through the back door he had to laugh silently at the idea. Shaving his head—that would be overkill.

◇◇◇

"Minstrel show?" Mad Dog said. "Oh, this isn't blackface. I'm Cheyenne and I'm painted because it helps me focus when I'm trying to contact the spirit world."

One of the men laughed. "We got our own contact with the spirit world right here." He drained a tall can and crushed it in his hand.

"Cheyenne, huh?" another said. His voice wasn't hostile, just curious. "I'm Cherokee."

"And I'm fucking Apache," said the one who'd accused Mad Dog of going to a minstrel show.

"No, really," the Cherokee said. "On my momma's side. She was a half-breed."

"Me too," Mad Dog said. "My mother always claimed to be half Cheyenne and half wildcat. She didn't live Cheyenne, though. Didn't know much about their ways. I had to find that out for myself."

The little group was silent for a minute, with only the first one muttering comments about wise-ass honkies to himself.

"I tried that," the Cherokee said. "Wouldn't nobody talk to a no account Black man like me. Seems we're considered inferior by Indians as well as everybody else."

"Got that right." It was one of the guys leaning on a fender.

"Always the black knight," somebody else said. A wise and thoughtful comment, and as unlikely in a group of post-mid-night street drinkers as a Cheyenne painted for a spirit quest or a sympathetic Cherokee.

"True," Mad Dog said. "The Cheyenne, they didn't want to talk to me at first. Especially after a little research showed mom was equal parts Cheyenne and Buffalo Soldier."

"Now you're shittin' me," Cherokee said.

"No, really," Mad Dog countered. "A sergeant in the 10th Cavalry was my great-granddaddy."

Nobody said anything to that.

"And," Mad Dog continued, "I got acquainted with a Choctaw once. Choctaw and Cherokee have a lot in common, since they're both members of the Five Civilized Tribes."

"I've heard that," Cherokee said.

"That Choctaw, he was dying," Mad Dog said. "I gave him a tree burial so Bonepicker and Buzzardman could clean the flesh off his bones before I put him in a burial mound."

"What bullshit." The first guy, the one who'd been looking for trouble from the start, had had enough.

"Shut up, man," Cherokee said. "He's right. I read up on it. That's the way it's got to be done, you want your soul to travel to the Milky Way like it's supposed to."

"The Milky Way," Mad Dog said, "is where my people go, too."

"Well fuck me, then," the trouble maker said. He tossed Mad Dog a sixteen-ouncer. "Sit down and tell us about your spirit world while you share some of ours."

Mad Dog, who limited himself to occasional beers or glasses of wine, popped the top on the malt liquor can. "Thanks," he said, and went over and sat by the guy who'd thrown him the drink. "That's real kind of you."

"I guess we're all brothers here," the man said.

Cherokee said, "That's a fact." After a general rumble of agreement from the rest of the men, he continued. "What else do you know about my people?"

"Not a lot," but Mad Dog figured he could always slip over into Cheyenne lore when he ran out of Chocktaw. And maybe these guys would let him use a telephone. Or give him a ride. Or just refrain from pounding the honky in blackface into a bloody pulp.

◇◇◇

The sheriff hadn't really thought this would work, so he didn't have a ready answer for Fig Zit's question. He had no idea who Fig Zit really was. But this god-like cartoon character didn't know who Madwulf was, either. And that might keep the conversation going. Maybe even tease some clue out of the monster.

"Ask him the same thing," the sheriff said. "Ask him who we are?"

Mrs. Kraus typed and the character threw his head back and laughed at her message.

"You're Harvey Edward Mad Dog," the voice boomed. "You're a sad old man from the middle of nowhere and I can kill you in reality as easily as I do here. As easily as I destroyed your home. As easily as I turned you into a murderer. You are nothing and I am all powerful."

"Not so all powerful as he thinks," the sheriff said. "Let's tell him so. Say, 'I am not Mad Dog.'"

Mrs. Kraus did it, and this time the character didn't respond. It just stood there, breathing deeply, occasionally rolling broad shoulders.

"That stopped him in his tracks," Mrs. Kraus said.

A bright pink message appeared at the bottom of their screen. "I guess you can't sleep any better without me than I can without you. Unless you're about to log off, I'll come help you run some quests."

The message was from a character named Pamdora.

"That pink," Mrs. Kraus said. "That's a whisper. Supposed to be a way for one character to talk to another without anyone else in the game knowing."

"You suppose that's Pam Epperson?" Pam was a young lady from Benteen County who'd left Kansas to play in a piano bar in Las Vegas, but not before starting an unlikely romance with the sheriff's brother.

"Makes sense," Mrs. Kraus said, "since she gave Mad Dog the game and got him started playing it."

"You can whisper back, right?"

Mrs. Kraus nodded.

"Just warn her then, 'trouble with Fig Zit.' Maybe she already knows about this guy."

Mrs. Kraus sent the reply, but just as she did, Fig Zit spoke again.

"Good morning, Mrs. Kraus," the creature said. "And Englishman, too, I presume."

◇◇◇

Heather peeked out the front window of Ms. Jardine's living room. The uniformed TPD officer who had followed them back to the house was still out there, parked in the driveway immediately behind Ms. Jardine's Prius. They might not be prisoners, but the police weren't planning to let them come and go without knowing about it.

Deputy Heather had called her dad and reported the circumstances. Live with it and get some sleep, her father said. Tomorrow might get hectic and he was working some angles back in Kansas. He'd keep her posted if anything important happened.

Ms. Jardine offered Heather a drink. Something to calm her down and help her get that sleep. Heather declined. Her host poured a glass of cabernet sauvignon for herself and curled up on one of her sofas. Heather was a little surprised not to be offered a hit on the bong that sat in front of the fireplace, but apparently it was there for decorative rather than functional reasons. It certainly fit the décor, which Heather decided was best described as delayed flower child. Paisleys and beaded curtains predominated.

Ms. Jardine lived just east of the university in a trendy neighborhood she laughingly referred to as Barrio Volvo. On the less desirable fringes, actually, where student rentals had become as common as owner-occupied properties. Parking was such a problem near the university, that Ms. Jardine had been forced to provide Heather with a guest permit to put in the front window of her rental car. That vehicle was right out front, not twenty feet from the police car. Getting out of the house wouldn't be a problem. It had a back door. A gate led to an alley behind. But Heather wasn't going to find another car in which she could go chasing after her uncle, not at this time of night. The only ones available to her were Jardine's Prius and her rental Kia. Both under the watchful eye of the officer parked in the driveway.

"You really should try to get some rest," Ms. Jardine said.

Heather wasn't interested. Not with Mad Dog the object of a citywide manhunt.

"I've got to go look for him," she insisted. Mad Dog was out there somewhere, on his own in a strange city. And a killer was on the loose. Worse yet, Captain Matus seemed convinced Mad Dog and the killer were one and the same. The Captain had seemed angry enough to bring in Mad Dog conveniently dead so all the troublesome problems of proving his guilt wouldn't be necessary.

Ms. Jardine listened sympathetically as Heather shared her worries. "I don't know how you expect to find him," she said. But, in the end, she agreed to help Heather slip TPD's surveillance.

A few minutes later, Heather exited the back door, used one wall of the house to block the policeman's view, and waited at the edge of the front yard for Ms. Jardine's grand performance. It came right on schedule. The front door flew open and Jardine ran down the driveway in a convincing state of hysterics. The cop leaped out of the car and she threw herself into his arms.

"Please help," Ms. Jardine cried. "Heather, she's gone."

"What?" the officer said. "How?"

"Out the back and down the alley. Come. Help me stop her. It's not safe for a young girl out there." Jardine dragged the cop up the driveway toward the back yard. The man resisted for a second, looking around as if deciding what to do.

"Hurry. I think we can still catch her."

That did it. The officer followed Jardine around the other side of the house and Heather slipped out of hiding and rushed to her rental. She fumbled with the unfamiliar lock and then slid behind the wheel. Ms. Jardine and the officer were still behind the house as she guided the car into the street and aimed it toward the nearest exit from the neighborhood.

Ms. Jardine had said Tucson covered something like two-hundred square miles. That was at least a thousand less than the jurisdiction she was used to working back in Kansas. Two-hundred square miles was hardly worth mentioning, she told herself. She didn't believe it, but at least she was out here. She had a chance.

◇◇◇

"How can Fig Zit know who we are?" Englishman asked.

Mrs. Kraus had an answer. "He's a hacker. The security on this game's pretty high, but I get people whispering to me about how I can buy gold or high-level equipment for cash all the time. This guy's just at another level."

"You're saying he's gotten into your account with War of Worldcraft?"

"Has to be."

"But how? You're not even playing your own character."

Mrs. Kraus threw her hands up in exasperation. "Hell, I'm no geek. I don't understand how this thing works. But Mad Dog and I turned out to be on the same server. It's not like Fig Zit had to sort through all the millions of people who play this game around the world. Or maybe he did. I don't know. But somehow he got into WOW's files and used some kind of program to find me. After that, guessing you're here would be easy."

"Only if he knows Benteen County," Englishman said.

"This has been interesting," Fig Zit said, "but I've wasted too much time on you little people. Prepare to die."

A pink message appeared in the bottom of the county's monitor. "Pam the Appalling, to the rescue—with dragons. Hurry back from the graveyard and help me kill him as he respawns."

"What do we do?" Englishman asked.

"Prepare to die, like he said," Mrs. Kraus said, typing madly. "Looks like Pam's rescue effort will fry us just as sure as Fig Zit's thunderbolts."

"Vampire wizards suck!" Mrs. Kraus' message appeared in a little bubble over Madwulf's head.

Fig Zit laughed. "Very funny, Mrs. Kraus. You are a...how does your generation put it? Oh yes, a caution. You almost make me hate to do this." The creature began rubbing his hands together, a sure sign he was about to cast a spell that would finish them.

"Here we go," Mrs. Kraus said. But she wasn't talking about the fate Fig Zit had in mind for them. She was pointing over the monster's shoulder at a figure astride a winged horse, and, just behind her, a host of monstrous flying lizards belching smoke and flames.

"Lordy," she said, "I think Pam's managed to bring Puff the Magic Dragon's Elite Reptilian Air Force."

Fig Zit hurled a flaming snowball and Madwulf's health all but disappeared. Not quite dead yet, Mrs. Kraus struck the monster with a double-bladed ax and smiled as Pam sailed by. It didn't stop Fig Zit from slamming them again, but, as Madwulf toppled, Puff and his army peeled off from their pursuit of Pam and began bathing the Vampire Wizard with their fiery breaths and rending him with scalpel-sharp teeth and claws.

"Watch," Mrs. Kraus said, pausing before sending Madwulf to the local graveyard again.

Fig Zit surprised her by killing five dragons and seriously damaging the last two before his corpse toppled and lay beside their own.

She hit the button and they were back at the cemetery, their spirit resurrected by the angel-like creature that resided there. They hadn't taken a dozen steps when Fig Zit's voice boomed out of the speakers once again.

"Damn you, Pamela Epperson. You should have minded your own business and had a good night's sleep in Las Vegas. Now I'm going to have to revenge myself on you, as well as some meddlesome folks in Benteen County. No more fun and games, little people. This ends now."

And, suddenly, they weren't in the magical forest of towering waterfall trees anymore. Their screen had flashed back to the log-in page where a message declared, "Server Down!"

"I think we pissed him off," Englishman said.

◇◇◇

The professional wasn't supposed to kill this one. Just make an impression, scare her. That didn't rule out a bit of maiming, he decided. Lopping off a few fingers with the hatchet, for instance, should accomplish his assigned task while sending the client a little message.

The back door opened on a dark utility room. Just beyond, he found a kitchen—clean, nearly scent free. It hadn't been cooked in lately. Next was a small dining room, and on its right, a living room that was more functional than ornamental. Not your run-of-the-mill woman living alone, he decided.

The living room was lit. A folded blue blazer lay on the arm of a wingback chair near the front door. A purse sat on the cushion and a cell phone was plugged in for recharging on an adjacent end table.

At the far end of the long narrow living room was an arch, like the one he'd passed through as he left the dining area. Opening on a hallway to bedrooms and baths, he decided. And someone was moving around back there. He could hear her coming his way. Her shadow appeared a moment before the light went out behind her. He launched himself toward where she was about to be—where she suddenly was.

She was handsome in a kind of formal manner, but not pretty. Her slacks had rigid starched pleats down the front of each leg. Her blouse was equally perfect and without wrinkles. But what caught his attention and stopped him in his tracks was the badge that was clipped to her belt, and the holstered pistol just behind it. His employer really should have told him she was a cop.

It was too far to cross the living room and get to her before she could draw her weapon. Maybe he could get back out through the dining room before she pulled it and fired. It would be close. Too close. That left one possibility.

"Mad Dog?" she whispered. At least the makeup had been effective and she wasn't going for the gun yet.

He smiled, half turned from her, and then came around with the hatchet. He threw it at the center of her chest. Getting away trumped fulfilling the terms of his contract. He wouldn't mind if his aim proved true, but he didn't stay to see the results. He had thrown axes before, but it wasn't one of his primary skills.

Instead, he used the throwing motion to pivot and dive back across the dining room toward the exit. When a bullet whined by his ear and took a chip out of the trim around a kitchen cabinet, he knew the ax had missed.

◇◇◇

The ax missed Parker's left hand by inches. By then, her right was full of SIG-Sauer. A nine mm slug tore into the elaborate woodwork just inside her kitchen but, like the ax, failed to hit its target. She followed him, moving fast, but not so fast as to go through that kitchen door without being sure he wasn't waiting just inside it, counting on her lack of caution.

The back door slammed. She went through the kitchen and the utility room and kicked the back door open. He was across the yard, swinging over her jagged fence top on the branch of an overhanging tree. She had a shot—one she would normally have taken—but behind him was a neighbor's house. The bedroom of a pair of pre-teen girls was just the other side of the spot where he landed. And then, as if he realized what was preventing her from firing, he was sprinting straight toward that home until a pair of garbage bins and an adobe wall gave him a chance to change directions and disappear from view.

"I thought you wanted to surrender to me," she called. A mockingbird was the only one to answer. She couldn't even hear his retreating footsteps.

Parker went back inside and grabbed a phone and paused at nine-one, not adding the final digit. Something bothered her. Something was wrong and she wasn't quite sure what.

She put the phone back in its cradle and returned to the living room. The ax had hit the wall head first and left a hole in her plaster, but it hadn't stuck. It lay on the floor and she went to it, knelt, and examined it without touching it.

Here was the problem, she realized. In the few times she'd seen Mad Dog decked out in his Cheyenne paraphernalia, he'd never been armed. No knife, no bow and arrow, certainly no ax. Nor had she ever heard of him carrying such things.

She bent, looked closer. Sighed.

She didn't know who had just tried to kill her, but it wasn't Harvey Edward Mad Dog. Of that, she was sure. This hatchet had a Wal-Mart price tag on the butt of the handle. Wal-Marts had doomed many small towns in rural America. She'd heard Mad Dog's rant on that subject often enough to know there was no way he'd use one of their products.

◇◇◇

"The fuck you doin'?"

Mad Dog thought the pretty black woman in the long t-shirt might calm down if she could have some malt liquor like the rest of them. He offered her his can but she didn't want it.

"And what's this crazy motherfucker with the black paint on his face doin' in my living room in the middle of the night?"

"He's not crazy," one of Mad Dog's new friends told her, neglecting the other epithet. "He's leading us in a kind of ceremony to help us get right with the spirits and shit."

"You already right with all the spirits you need," she said, "way you slurring your words."

"I'm sorry we woke you." Mad Dog thought he really should have argued against group drumming, but their host had that African drum right there in the living room.

"Aw, honey," the man said. "Calm down now. What we're doing here's important. This man, he's a shaman and he's got himself some trouble. If we help him, maybe we can help ourselves, too."

"I'll shaman your ass, you don't get these no-goods out of my house this very minute."

"We don't really need the drum," Mad Dog said. "We could just sit in a circle and be quiet and focus on the spirit world."

The woman stalked across the room and bent over and put her face inches from Mad Dog's.

"What part of 'out' don't you understand, Mr. Shaman?"

"I guess we *should* go," Cherokee said.

The circle of friends stood, none too steady, and reached out to help Mad Dog to his feet.

"Is gettin' kinda late," one said.

"My wife will be on me like black on rice, I don't get my ownself home," another agreed.

The group found themselves on the front porch, the door slammed behind them almost before they knew it.

"You need a ride?" Cherokee asked Mad Dog.

"Yeah," he said, "only I don't know where."

"That's okay," Cherokee said. "I'm probably too drunk to find it, anyway. And I sure don't need to be getting no DUI." He handed Mad Dog his keys. "That red Chevy over there. You drive and we'll take a couple of these drunk brothers home."

"I don't know," Mad Dog said. He was a little woozy himself, though he'd just begun his second can of malt.

"You'll be fine," Cherokee said. "Besides, after what you told us, if the man stops us, he ain't gonna breathalize you. Hell, cop killer like you—they'll shoot you dead before you can get outta the car."

◇◇◇

Both lines to the Benteen County Sheriff's office rang simultaneously. The sheriff nodded to Mrs. Kraus. "Looks like we're on duty early today," he said. He maneuvered his walker over to his desk while Mrs. Kraus got the first line. He picked up the second and said, "Sheriff English."

"Hi, Daddy." It was Heather. "Guess what I did?"

He didn't feel like guessing and didn't get the chance when Mrs. Kraus held up her phone and told him, "Tucson Police Department for you."

"Can you hang on, honey?" he asked. "I've got an official call on the other line."

"I may know what that's about," she said, "but go ahead and take it. It might save me some explaining."

He didn't like the sound of that, but he put her on hold and punched the button for the other line.

"I thought we had an agreement to cooperate on this investigation," a voice said. He didn't recognize it. It wasn't one of the detectives he'd talked to before. Nor was it that Sewa Police captain.

He'd opened his end of the conversation the same way he'd answered his daughter's call. "I identified myself. Perhaps you could extend me the same courtesy."

"This is Deputy Chief Dempsey, Tucson Police Department. Acting chief at the moment, until the regular chief gets back from a conference. I'm told we had an agreement. You'd do what you could to talk your brother into surrendering and we wouldn't hold your daughter if she'd stay with the Jardine woman."

"That's correct." The sheriff thought he knew why Heather was calling now.

"That doesn't seem to be working on this end. Your daughter made a run for it and got away."

"Do you plan to charge her?"

"Not yet. But we can change that, put out a warrant if she doesn't turn herself back in, and damn soon."

The sheriff nodded. "I see."

"Then there's another matter," Dempsey said. "You suggested your brother might be willing to surrender to our Sergeant Parker."

"I intend to suggest it to him when he calls back. He hasn't done that yet."

Dempsey's tone made it clear he didn't believe the sheriff. "Sergeant Parker had a visitor a few minutes ago. A man covered in black body paint with white lightning bolts on his arms, legs and face. He broke into her house and tried to kill her with a hatchet."

"Mad Dog would never do that." Even as he denied the possibility, the sheriff wondered if his brother could have gotten into some bad peyote or screwed up a joke on Parker, not that Mad Dog knew where she lived.

"Funny," Dempsey said. "Sergeant Parker also says it couldn't have been him. But I'll tell you what I told her. Even a city the size of Tucson is going to have a limited number of whacked-out, body-painted shamans running around assaulting people with edged weapons on any given night. That's why I issued an armed and dangerous warning to my people a few minutes ago, along with an order to use all necessary force. You understand me?"

"Shoot first, ask later. Yeah," the sheriff said, "that's clear enough."

"You deliberately overstate my orders, Sheriff English, but if you want to see your brother taken alive, you better inform him to just stop, wherever he is, lie face down with his arms and legs spread so it's clear he's no threat, and not move while you notify us where to find him before we do it ourselves."

"I will, Chief Dempsey, if he calls back. You've got his cell phone so I can't contact him. He hasn't called me since I talked to your detectives." The sheriff purposefully left off mentioning that his daughter was holding on the other line.

"Then you better hope to hear from him *real* soon," Dempsey said. "Because we *will* find him, and we *will not* let him get away from us again."

There was suddenly a dial tone humming in the sheriff's ear. He glanced at Mrs. Kraus and gave her a "not good" shake of the head as he punched onto the other line.

"Heather," he said. "I hope to hell you ran because you're with your uncle or know where he is. If not, they may be issuing a shoot-on-site order for you pretty soon, like the one they just put out on him."

The second line was quiet for a moment. Then Heather said, "No, Daddy. I haven't a clue. I hoped you'd tell me where to look for him."

◇◇◇

After they dropped off the last rider, Cherokee directed Mad Dog through a few blocks of neighborhood, then told him to turn north on Grande.

"That over there," Cherokee explained, "used to be Dunbar School. It's where all the Black kids went back when Tucson was segregated."

"Arizona had segregated schools?" Mad Dog hadn't thought of this as part of the Old South.

"Yep. And on your left is Estevan Park. It had the only pool colored kids could use. You know who Estevan was?"

Mad Dog was considering the question when Cherokee told him to turn east on Speedway.

"Estevan the Moor was a slave. Part of Cabeza de Vaca's party, the first Europeans to enter this country."

Mad Dog remembered. The Indians had considered Estevan a great sorcerer, too great to live when he led the way into Cibola ahead of Fray Marcos de Niza.

"And Tucson was part of the Confederacy in the Civil War," Cherokee continued. "Lots of Southern sympathizers here back then, until the California Column marched across the desert and drove the Rebs out. Say, I bet you didn't know the farthest west battle of the Civil War took place just north of here near I-10—place called Picacho Peak."

Cherokee continued the history lesson as he directed Mad Dog east and north.

"I live in Sugar Hill," the man said, "where rich Negroes moved while white folks got out of their way and beat it for the foothills. Wife and I, we got an apartment in this complex, just over here."

It looked like a nice place with tall palms and neatly manicured vegetation. Mad Dog pulled in and Cherokee opened his door and climbed out, even though Mad Dog couldn't see any vacant parking places.

"You can leave the car in the street, just down from the park there," he said. "Let me go smooth the way for you with my old lady. We're in two-oh-four, second floor on the left."

Mad Dog watched to see which set of stairs his new friend took, then backed out onto the street and headed for where he'd been told to park. He chose a spot behind a white van. As he pulled in, the van suddenly accelerated out of its spot. Metal slammed metal as it encountered the vehicle in front and broken glass rained into the street. Mad Dog wasn't thrilled with the idea of talking to the van's driver while his face and hands were still covered in black body paint. Or with the inevitable call to police to investigate the accident. But the van had hit hard enough that someone could be hurt in there.

He opened his door and got ready to begin trying to explain himself. No one wanted to hear. All the doors on the van flew open and people began running every direction.

"What the…?" Mad Dog uttered.

For the longest time, no one answered. He walked into the street where the Chevy's headlamps illuminated the damage, then went to the van's sliding door and peered inside. It smelled of people and sweat and fear in there. A small voice addressed him from the darkness.

"Are you *la migra*?"

He couldn't see her at first, for all the bags of clothing and jugs of water that had been left behind by the mass exodus.

"*La migra*?"

"Immigration," she explained. She stepped forward from the back of the van—very young with long dark hair. "The coyote, our smuggler," she said, "he saw you drive by, then turn around in the parking lot down the street and come back. He said you were Immigration and we would try to outrun you, only he panicked and lost control."

She had her arms wrapped around herself. Though she was tiny and slight, he realized she was also very pregnant.

"Are you all right?"

"When we hit, our coyote, he told everyone, 'Run! Save yourselves!' But I couldn't. I hit my head. I'm still…. How do you say it? A little wobbly."

She stumbled over something in the dark and fell forward. He caught her and her big dark eyes peered up into his.

"If you're not Immigration," she said, "why wear all that camouflage paint?"

◇◇◇

Captain Matus wasn't surprised when Heather ran. He'd been expecting it. In fact, once he got used to the idea that TPD was going to let her go home with Ms. Jardine—under watch—he'd been counting on it. He'd set up an observation post a block from the residence where he could keep an eye on the most likely exits from the building. Then he'd sat and sipped coffee and listened to the scanner, waiting for a report of the girl making a break for it.

He saw it happen about when he'd expected. Long enough for whoever was on watch to settle in and get comfy. Long enough to believe she might have gone to sleep. But not so long as to let Tucson begin to wake up.

There was no doubt in his mind that Heather English was covering for her uncle. Maybe she didn't believe the man was a killer, he'd grant her that, but he was sure she knew where Mad Dog was, or where he was likely to go. And Matus was sure, if she slipped past TPD's watch at the house, she'd lead him right to the man who'd murdered his officer.

TPD scrambled units to look for Heather English. But by then she was in her car and on the street. She'd even, cleverly, slipped into another neighborhood to make sure she wasn't being followed. Matus pulled into the same neighborhood a couple of blocks later. Then he asked his cousin where she was going. His cousin worked for the car rental company Heather English had used when she arrived in Tucson. Over the years, and this close to the border, the firm had discovered it was a good idea to install GPS devices in their cars. His cousin was an assistant manager. Actually, considering how complicated the Sewa godparent relationship system was, Matus was related, one way or another, to nearly every member of the tribe.

As a favor, and it was always a good idea to be owed a favor by a captain on the tribal police force, his cousin had gone to the office and was monitoring the GPS on the English girl's car. That way, all Matus had to do was sit and listen to his cousin's instructions on the cell phone. He followed her out of the second neighborhood a mile north of where she'd entered it. After that, she went west, down Grant Road, back toward Pascua Village.

She pulled over in a shopping center along the way. He continued past on Grant, turning at the next stoplight in the direction he thought she might take. She was parked close enough to one of the lights in the empty grocery store's parking lot that he could see she was making a cell phone call. To her uncle, he hoped. Arranging a place to meet.

A few minutes later, he was back on Grant and heading west again. Her tail lights were far ahead, or, what his cousin told him had to be her tail lights. She surprised him by how close to Pascua she went. He hadn't thought Mad Dog would be anywhere near the scene of the crime.

Her car stopped several blocks south of Grant, just off Oracle. It was near the sex shop Mad Dog had stopped at after the murder. Matus dropped down a side street that would intercept the one she was on and turned off his headlights while he was still a couple of blocks away.

He drove slowly after that—cautious not to encounter a drunken pedestrian or another car proceeding without lights. The neighborhood was mixed use, everything from low-grade industrial to cheap apartments. This long after "last call" in all the city's bars, the area was dead. Nothing moved. There weren't many lights in the residences he passed. He only saw one sign of life, a scruffy coyote, desperate enough after the long dry winter to extend its hunting range far inside the city limits.

Matus pulled to a stop half a block short of the intersection where his cousin reported the girl was parked. He had disabled his dome light earlier, so nothing but the sound of the door opening and closing could give him away. Alley or street? He was still considering when Heather English appeared in the glow of the streetlight that had nearly persuaded him to take the alley. He ducked behind a dumpster, a good thing, since she stopped in the middle of the street and looked in every direction. Then she opened her mouth and threw her head back and howled like a wolf. The coyote he'd seen yipped a reply and a few distant dogs barked. Way off, something deep and eerie echoed her more accurately.

Was that a signal? Was this an attempt to find her uncle and his wolf-dog? He had no idea. Before he managed to come up with any other possibilities, she began jogging down the center of the street, heading east.

Matus couldn't follow her in his car, not after she'd abandoned hers. That would be too obvious. It didn't take long for him to regret his choice of footwear tonight. His custom-made cowboy boots with the fancy stitching were wonderfully comfortable for standing or riding, but these boots weren't made for walking the way Nancy Sinatra's had been in that long ago hit song. And they sure as hell weren't made for jogging across Tucson.

◇◇◇

"I believe I can keep you employed for the foreseeable future," the professional's client said.

"Oh?" The client was a major problem. The man had found him when he shouldn't be findable. And the man had failed to provide him with crucial information—sending him to scare a cop without knowing she was one. What other information might not be delivered? On the other hand, the longer the client kept him working and stayed in touch, the easier it would be to back track him. The professional already had people working on that.

The client failed to note the chill response his announcement received, or didn't care. "This Mad Dog operation, it's turned much more complicated than it started out."

For the professional, as well. He had expected to be on an airplane to the Cayman Islands by now.

"There are some people in Kansas I want you to punish for me. And one in Las Vegas."

"In what fashion?"

"Some unpleasant and memorable incident. I'm not sure I want them killed, but I want them to suffer."

"I can arrange something." That part might be enjoyable, but he had already set the wheels in motion. His researchers would find out who this client was. As soon as they did, he'd cease fulfilling contracts for the man and begin a personal operation against him.

"And the good part is you can start right there in Tucson, while you're seeing that Mad Dog isn't taken alive."

"What do you have in mind?"

"Mad Dog has a brother."

The professional knew that. He'd found out as part of his inquiries as he prepared for the original job. He didn't say anything, though, and the client continued. "A half-brother, actually, but they're close. Mad Dog's death will hurt him, but I want him to suffer more."

Ah, the professional thought. The daughter, Heather. Yes, this might be interesting.

"He has a daughter visiting Tucson now. She has managed to slip the loose reconnaissance the police had on her and is missing—presumably, searching for her uncle. Do you think you can find her?"

"Yes, I think I can manage that." He'd watched her jog into that deserted intersection and stop to howl only a few moments before. That he was close to her was a pleasant coincidence. He'd decided the best way to get to Mad Dog was to let Captain Matus do the finding. So he'd used one of his many resources to discover the Sewa had staked out the house where the girl was staying. And, after that, where she led him. Cops never expected to be followed. Trailing the Captain as he tracked the English girl had been simple. Now his new target was trotting down empty streets just a few blocks away.

"What do you want me to do to her?"

The client laughed. "Something humiliating and painful," he said. And then he became very specific in a way that surprised even the professional.

"Done. What do I need to know about her?" The client had already failed to mention that her father was a sheriff. She was some kind of honorary deputy. His question was a test of whether the client would supply that information. The professional should be told when any target was in law enforcement.

"Her name is Heather English. She's smart, she's attractive. Do you need a picture of her?"

"No." So, the client would continue to edit relevant data. No surprise, but more reason to find him sooner rather than later. "I already know what the girl looks like. I saw her at Pascua."

"Good. How soon might I expect results on this? And on Mad Dog? I'll pay a twenty percent bonus over your usual fee if the girl is taken care of before dawn."

"Thirty percent and I'll do it within the hour."

"Done," the client said. And, before he hung up, "Enjoy yourself."

The professional intended to. Heather English was a very attractive young woman. Not that attractive young women aroused him. Their pain and fear—now that was another matter.

◇◇◇

Sheriff English had told Heather to turn herself in. He knew she wouldn't, though she hadn't come right out and admitted that. It was why he told her where Mad Dog had been when he called, and how long ago. If the only way she'd turn herself in to the police was with, and assuring the safety of, her uncle, then maybe helping her disobey would get both of them out of danger. He didn't know.

It was tough, being half a continent away from the action, and hardly able to get around because of his spinal injury. Especially since there was so little he could think of to do at this hour. Hardly anyone was up and about in Kansas or Arizona to help him find people, even if he figured out who he should find and how they could assist.

As the sheriff made three calls in a row to Pam Epperson in Las Vegas, and found the line busy each time, Mrs. Kraus used the other line to throw questions at someone from the company that owned War of Worldcraft. Surely, if anyone could tell them who was hacking their system, it was WOW. But, Mrs. Kraus had told him it was slow going. First, she was switched from person to person, and that only after she finally succeeded in getting a real human being on the line. WOW didn't keep many decision makers on duty in the wee hours, they told her. And, so far, that had proved true. She hadn't found anyone with the authority to give her any information. The angry young man she had on the line now—the tech trying to bring their server back online—had said he should hear from a supervisor soon. He didn't much care about the legal niceties himself. He just wanted to find the hacker who'd brought the game down—that, and keep his job.

While Mrs. Kraus argued, the sheriff dug through files until he found a recent number for Deputy Parker—Sergeant Parker, back down there in Tucson. She was the best deputy he'd had in all his years as sheriff. When she applied for a Benteen County job he'd known she was running from something. No way someone with her skills would take a low-paying job in rural Kansas otherwise.

He'd checked to see what it was, of course. She'd done her best in a terrible situation during her first stint in Tucson, but a hostage died because she wasn't clairvoyant. The sheriff hired her, knowing the odds. The guilt might wash her out, even in Central Kansas. Or she'd find a way to work through it. If that happened, she'd move back where they supported law enforcement with technology and decent salaries. Either way, he'd known she was temporary. Invaluable, though, since facing her demons had put her in a situation where she saved his daughters' lives at the same time.

Finding Parker's number didn't help, since her line was busy the first time he called it, then there was no answer.

"Sergeant Parker should be back in soon," an officer in Tucson told him when he called the department's headquarters. "You want to leave a message on her voice mail?"

The sheriff asked the man to have her call him as soon as possible. He tried Pam again and the line was still busy. English hung up his phone and wondered what to do next. He was thinking about joining Mrs. Kraus in her conversation with the WOW tech, but he didn't even understand most of her side of the exchange. He knew he'd be hopeless with the geek on the other end.

The free line rang and he grabbed it.

"Englishman, it's me, Pam Epperson. I've been trying to get in touch with Mad Dog and he's not answering and now someone who claims to be a cop in Tucson has his cell and the guy started demanding I tell him how to find Mad Dog. I hung up on him. What's going on? Is Mad Dog all right?"

The sheriff gave her the short version—rushed trip to join Heather for the Easter ceremonies at Pascua, murdered officer, Mad Dog on the run and out of contact while, back in Kansas, Mad Dog's house had been destroyed by a grenade launcher.

"But he was playing War of Worldcraft with me just a few minutes ago," Pam said.

"That was me," the sheriff said, "or Mrs. Kraus, with me making suggestions. See, Mad Dog called after the killing in Tucson. He's got some weird theory…"

"That Fig Zit's escaped from the game and is trying to get at Mad Dog for real."

The sheriff had expected to have to sell her that one, not find her arguing Mad Dog's case before he could even explain it.

"I'll be on the next plane to Tucson," Pam said, as if she thought you could find someone as easily in a metropolitan area of a million people as you could back home in Buffalo Springs.

"Don't…" the sheriff started to tell her.

"I'll stay in touch," Pam said.

Mrs. Kraus' monitor flashed—dazzling colors, then a scene from back in the game swirled into focus. Fig Zit's features leered from the screen. "I'll teach you to meddle," his voice roared. The sheriff could hear an echo over Pam's phone. It must be on her computer, too. "My revenge begins now. On each of you—Pam Epperson, Mrs. Kraus, Sheriff English. You first, Sheriff. I want you to know that right now, I'm turning one of my demons loose on your daughter in Tucson."

"Jesus," the sheriff muttered. How did the bastard know Heather wasn't safely under house arrest in Tucson? How did he even know she was in Arizona?

"Oh no," Pam whispered. "Tell Mad Dog I'm on the way." And then a dial tone hummed in the sheriff's ear. Not that he noticed right away because Fig Zit had one more thing to say.

"The monster I'm sending, he won't kill her," the creature growled. "But after the things he does to her, she'll wish he had."

◇◇◇

Mad Dog ushered the pregnant girl to Cherokee's Chevy. She'd told him she was feeling better and he didn't need to help her or take her anywhere, but standing in the headlight's glare, he'd noticed she had quite a bump on her forehead. As he held the door for her, he tried to explain about being a Cheyenne shaman, and that was why his face was painted.

"You through doing the shaman thing," she asked as he got behind the wheel and pulled into the street, "or do you want to keep the paint on?"

"Through," he conceded. She pulled a soft cloth and a plastic water jug out of her backpack and started gently scrubbing his face.

He halted at a stop sign at the first corner and paused.

"Where are we going, Señor Shaman?"

"I don't suppose you know how to find a hospital?"

"Oh sure," she said. "I've lived more of my life in Tucson than Mexico. Closest one is probably University Hospital. That's almost due east, but really, you don't need to take me there. I'm fine."

"I'll feel a lot better about it if you get that bump looked at. Head injuries can seem like nothing and then the brain starts swelling and…. Well, I'd just rather you get it looked at."

"I can't pay," she said, moving her attentions from his cheeks to his forehead. The paint seemed to be washing off easily. This stuff must be better quality than he got from that sex shop in Wichita.

"With the new border security, it cost me everything I had to pay the coyote to get me across."

"I'll pay for your treatment," he said. "How much can it be?"

She shook her head. "You Cheyenne, you don't go to emergency rooms much, do you?"

He admitted he'd never been treated in one himself.

"I mean," she said, "I don't know exactly, but I think this could cost a thousand dollars. Maybe more."

He didn't believe her. Oh, he'd heard horror stories about medical costs and insurance coverage on the news. But this was just a bump. If he'd taken her to Doc Jones back in Kansas, there wouldn't even be a charge.

Mad Dog only had a couple of hundred in cash, but he had credit cards. He started to tell her but she was speaking again.

"Emergency rooms here, they'll treat people whether they have money or not. You should just drop me off at the entrance and then go on your way. I don't want to be an even bigger burden."

"No way. I won't just abandon you." For one thing, he wasn't sure she'd go inside if he left her. For another, he had no intention of making this hospital or the taxpayers pick up the bill when he was the one who'd taken responsibility for her. The coyote, that was the guy who should pay. But the smuggler wasn't available.

What would he do with her after she'd been treated? He hadn't worked that part out yet. She'd admitted she was here illegally, but could he turn her in? Would he have crossed a border, just the way she had, whether trying for a better life was legal or not? He couldn't say.

"Turn here," she told him. It was a big street. Wide and empty and well lit. And there was a huge complex of buildings ahead. A sign said EMERGENCY.

She started working on the paint on his hand, the one she could reach. "You are a very kind man," she said. "I don't think I've ever met anyone quite like you."

He grinned a foolish grin. There was probably no way he could make himself turn her in. And then her grip on his hand went from gentle to savage. He thought she was going to squeeze straight through to the bone.

"What…" he said.

"The baby," she said. "I think he comes now."

◇◇◇

Heather English knew she was being followed. Her law enforcement training might be limited—mostly watching her dad at work as she grew up, then, on very rare occasions, lending a hand. But her pursuer's leather soles made noise when they slapped on pavement, or tried to be quieter and ran along the sandy edges of the street. She thought about just outrunning him, but she was curious. Had TPD set her up in the hopes she'd lead them to Uncle Mad Dog?

A vacant house with boarded windows was just ahead. Sections of the low picket fence along the street had collapsed, and there was a big tree in the front yard that shaded part of the pavement. She jogged into the shadows, dodging patches of weeds, and threw a look over her shoulder. The owner of those leather soles wasn't visible, though she could still hear him. She ran behind the empty house and circled it, spooking a mangy coyote on the way, and found a good hiding place behind a cluster of dying cactus. From there, she could watch for her pursuer and still have a choice of escape routes.

Except he didn't come. And, by the time she got around the house, she couldn't hear his footsteps anymore. She waited, sure he hadn't seen where she went, even if he somehow knew she'd stopped. She waited some more. Nothing happened. No one came. No more footsteps, stealthy or otherwise. Just the whisper of the breeze through moonlit vegetation and the ceaseless hum of a city that never fully slept.

She went back around the house, moving soft and quiet. She could get a better view back down the street from there, but it didn't help. Nothing moved out there. Nothing out of the ordinary, except….

What was that? Back down by the corner. When she came this way, she'd run along that side of the street and there hadn't been a heap of rags at the edge of the road. She waited a bit longer but it didn't move. Nothing moved. Heather crept through the shadows, back into the street. Still nothing. Nothing but that unfamiliar roadside lump.

Curiosity kills, she told herself, but she couldn't keep from retracing her steps, from finding out what that was and why she hadn't noticed it.

It got her adrenaline up, but she wasn't afraid. Her dad had begun teaching her hand-to-hand self defense as soon as she was big enough to walk. Since she'd gone off to college, she'd filled her exercise time with classes in all sorts of martial arts. They were great exercise regimes and they'd helped her cope with her mother's losing battle with cancer. She was sure she'd be better than whoever might be back there.

The bundle of rags had a hand. The hand was attached to an arm that reached from the gravel to the edge of the pavement. This was a person! One who hadn't been here when she passed. Was he hurt? Dead? Faking it to catch her off guard?

The hand was motionless. As she got closer, she could see that the heap had a face. Its mouth drooled into the dirt. A nose oozed blood. She prodded him with a foot, ready to skip back if he made a grab for her, or maybe stomp that hand. Her prod got no reaction.

She circled him. He wore leather soles on expensive western boots. She remembered the elaborate stitching.

"Captain Matus?"

When he didn't answer, she circled behind him and approached from where he'd have the most trouble grabbing her, from where she'd have the best chance of making him pay if he did. She bent, got a handful of hair, and lifted his face. It was Matus, all right, and breathing, but out cold. With some fresh road rash on his face, too, as if he'd suddenly lost consciousness and gone down head first into the gravel.

"Captain," she said it louder this time, shaking him a little. The blood that dripped from his nose was her only answer.

And then a soft voice spoke from across the street as a shadowy form materialized from behind a trash bin.

"Hello, Heather English," the voice said. "Meeting you like this, it's going to be my pleasure."

◇◇◇

She pleased the professional.

She didn't scream. She didn't flinch—not even when her cell phone rang. He liked the tough ones, the ones who wouldn't show you their fear. When they broke, they had so much farther to fall. Their suffering could be truly exquisite.

He wasn't quite so pleased when she bounced to her feet on the far side of the unconscious captain and assumed a defensive stance—taekwondo, he thought. One more thing the client hadn't seen fit to mention. She let her phone chirp, unanswered, keeping her hands curled in tight fists just where they should be in order to defend herself.

He needed to talk to his resources. See if they had any leads back to his client yet. He really should have checked with them before starting this particular contract. But what the client wanted done to the girl had the potential to be wonderfully gratifying.

"Who are you?" she said. "How do you know my name? What happened to Captain Matus?"

"I happened to Matus." He advanced across the street, slow, casual, only his words threatening. "I'm your destiny, Heather. And I know your name because someone wanted us to meet."

She took a couple of steps back. Cautious ones, and she glanced around, choosing her ground and considering escape routes.

"The captain will be fine," he said. "I am an expert at pressure points and blows that stun. The good captain should wake in ten or fifteen minutes and be hardly the worse for wear."

When she'd moved, she kept her hands up and her feet properly spaced. But, after all, how good could she be, this little girl from the Kansas sticks? And it didn't really matter, even if she were some expert with a black belt. He just hoped she wasn't so good that he'd have to kill her rather than enjoy the things the client wanted.

He got to Matus and stepped around him. He was close to her, now. Close enough to be on her and overpower her in seconds. Unless she was truly skilled. Better to test that. Better to know how seriously to take her before taking her the way he had in mind. He decided to show her a target. The switchblade snapped open in his hand—six inches of razor sharp steel that gleamed, reflecting the moon and distant street lights.

"I'll start by taking your nipples," he said. "And then there's a form of scalping you may not have heard of. It takes the pubic hair and a circle of flesh from between your legs. White men used to perform the operation on Indian squaws, you know. They wore the resulting trophies as hat bands."

She fell back two more steps with the shock of what he told her. Somewhere, far away, he heard a siren, and, perhaps, a wolf's howl. And, had she just growled at him?

"Then, I think, we'll perform a minor surgery that will further affect your future sex life, if any. Are you familiar with female circumcision?"

He thrust the knife and her foot came up to kick it but he spun and kicked her leg and knocked her off balance. Not quite badly enough for her to fall. Not quite enough to leave her open to the attack he'd planned. She wasn't bad, he thought. Or she was very lucky.

"I didn't think I wanted to hurt you," the girl said. "Now, I'll enjoy it." And she came for him—kick, kick, a block to his counter strike. She even landed a blow on his knife hand that left it numb and tingling.

Much better than he'd expected. Before she could recover and attack again, he went at her—kick, spin, kick, palm strike with the hand without the knife because she wouldn't expect that. She blocked the kicks. The palm strike caught her solidly in the sternum and sent her tumbling into a thick copse of desert broom. It swallowed her completely and she must have landed badly because he heard a yelp as she fell—a kind of panicked, inhuman cry.

He went in after her. Something with fur and teeth launched itself from the brush. Jaws snapped and he danced back. He couldn't retreat fast enough. Teeth closed on his left hand. The pain was incredible. He used the knife—snick, snick—and the thing died, teeth still buried in his hand. But the girl wasn't in the bush anymore. She was up and running. She had a half-block lead on him and he was still locked in the death grip of a mangy coyote.

◇◇◇

"No answer," the sheriff said as Heather's phone cycled to her message box. He put his own phone back in its cradle.

"Don't mean nothin'." Mrs. Kraus pushed her chair away from the computer. "Just 'cause he says something's going to happen to her, don't mean it will."

"I know," the sheriff said, "but Mad Dog was convinced it was him, Fig Zit, right there in Tucson killing that cop and getting Mad Dog blamed for it."

"You aren't usually so quick to accept your brother's screwball theories."

She was right, there. It was just that he was so far away. So unable to protect his daughter if she needed it. And unable to even find out if the threat was real.

"You saw that?" Mrs. Kraus said. It took the sheriff a moment to realize she was talking to the War of Worldcraft tech on her own phone. "He did, he saw it," she told the sheriff. "One of the most powerful hacks he's ever encountered, but it left tracks he says. He's tracing them. Put me on hold while he runs them down."

"Does he think he can find Fig Zit?"

She nodded. "Unless Fig Zit really is some kind of magical character living in their machines. I think he was joking when he said that part."

And then she was clearly listening again, the very picture of rapt attention. "It was from our time zone, he says. And a node on the net with only a few dozen players. But beamed by satellite. They're all off line now, so he can't tell for sure which one of them did it."

"Can he give us the list of those subscribers?" the sheriff asked.

"Says he'll have to look 'em up."

"But he can tell us where they are? What city? What neighborhood, maybe?"

"Middle of nowhere, he says."

"And where's that?"

"Damn," she said. "It's right here."

"Buffalo Springs?"

"Yeah, but bigger. Parts of the Plains, all the way from Canada to Texas, with us included."

"How many here? How many right here in Buffalo Springs or Benteen County? Can he tell us that?"

She shook her head. "Not until he can dig into the subscription records. And he says he's not allowed to give that kind of information out."

The sheriff reached down and picked up his phone, punching onto the same line Mrs. Kraus was using.

"This is Sheriff English," he told the man. "I know there are legal procedures that should be followed, but you saw him, right? You heard what he threatened to do to my daughter. What you tell me could keep her alive."

He could practically hear the gears turning in the tech's head as the man mulled it over. "Okay," the guy finally said. "I'll do it. But I've got to access those records from another computer. I'll put you on hold and be right back."

"Hot damn," Mrs. Kraus hooted. Her smile vanished as the line went dead. The windows turned bright and shards of glass came flying into the office from the explosion that rocked the front of the building.

◇◇◇

The professional pried the dead coyote's jaws open and dug its canines from his flesh. He checked his hand for damage as the animal crumpled to the ground at his feet. The damage was painful, but not major. Still, he should see a doctor if for no other reason than a coyote, foolish enough to hunt in the heart of the city, might well be rabid. But he wanted the girl, now, worse than ever. His targets didn't get away from him.

He considered it. He could probably still catch her, though she was more than a block ahead of him already. But it would take time and she could raise enough of a clamor so that the best he'd be able to achieve would be a quick kill. That wasn't what the client wanted, and now it wasn't what the professional wanted, either. So she'd have to wait. He turned and began jogging back to his car.

The client had failed to provide necessary information yet again. The girl wasn't just some back-country hick-deputy. She was highly skilled. He should have known that going in.

He took a short detour on the way to his car, going by hers long enough to let the air out of two tires. Not that she'd be back for it soon. He'd put a good scare into her. She was probably still running.

Once in his car, he pulled a cell phone out of his back pocket, activated it, and dialed as he pulled away from the curb.

"How can I help," a voice said. Sometimes at this company he had to leave a message or wait for a call back, but when that happened, or when it was answered, he always spoke to the same voice. The professional wasn't so sure it was always the same person. You could do so much with electronic voice alteration these days. He had used many information technology firms during his career. This was his favorite. He'd found it a few months ago on an internet chat room where unusual business arrangements were the rule. You had to know how to find the place and use some caution to be sure you weren't negotiating with law enforcement officers setting up a sting, but he'd made several valuable contacts there, including his current troublesome client. Considering what this firm researched for him, it must know he was involved with people who died violent deaths. The voice never expressed concern when he paid well, and he paid very well indeed. In fact, it seemed to have adjusted to his peculiar needs.

"Have you managed to backtrack my client?"

"No, sir. Not yet. He's built a complex web of false identities. We're weeding through them. This may take a few hours."

The professional knew this firm could not be hurried. They always performed at maximum efficiency. If the voice said it couldn't be done yet, it couldn't.

"Signal me at all possible contact points as soon as you have an answer."

"Of course," the voice said, and the professional realized that wasn't an issue he'd needed to raise. They would get the word to him the moment they knew.

"I need to find a trauma doctor."

"Is this an emergency?"

"No," the professional said, "but sooner is better."

"Privately and without record?"

They did understand his needs. He agreed that an undocumented transaction would be preferred and the voice put him on hold for a moment as he cruised slowly north on Oracle. Matus should be coming around soon and the professional hadn't even bothered to see if the Sewa policeman was armed. He hadn't taken the time because the girl might have looked around and realized a second person was following her. That could have scared her enough to call for local police help. Now, it made no sense for him to stay in that neighborhood. If he went back, it would be when he could make full use of both hands, or near it. He would go after her again, but on his own terms.

"The University of Arizona Medical Center," the voice said, and gave him an address. "Do you need directions?"

"No," he said. "But isn't that a rather public place?"

"A nurse will be waiting for you just outside the emergency room entrance. He'll be wearing blue scrubs and will have an unlit cigarette in his mouth. You'll tell him you are the client referred by Fick Internet Technologies. He'll see that your visit to one of the city's finest trauma surgeons occurs with the degree of privacy you require."

"Good. Then I want a dossier on Heather English, Kansas University law student and Benteen County Deputy Sheriff. Go as deep as you can in order for me to have it in an hour."

"Emphasis?" the voice asked.

"Strengths, weaknesses," the professional said. "Motivation. The usual."

"It will be done."

He didn't say anything else before disconnecting. He knew what he wanted would be ready in precisely sixty minutes. He turned right at the next stoplight and headed for the hospital, or its vicinity. To be on the safe side, he would park in a nearby neighborhood and walk to his meeting with the nurse. This rental car had already spent too long near crime scenes. If anyone should look for him at the hospital, there was no sense leaving them a trail. But he wouldn't walk too far, he thought. With the imposed travel restriction he'd put on the girl by slashing her tires, and the information Fick would provide, he hoped to resume his relationship with Heather English soon after he left the hospital. It was something to look forward to.

◇◇◇

The psycho didn't follow her so Heather made a wide, cautious circle. This guy was very dangerous. He hadn't looked like a Native American, but somehow, she felt sure she'd just run into the man Uncle Mad Dog said had killed the Sewa policeman. What other stranger in Tucson would know who she was? If this had only been some local neighborhood nut, he couldn't have named her and he probably wouldn't have described the tortures he had in mind for her quite so lovingly. No, there was something personal about it for this guy. Something seriously sick.

She set her cell to vibrate as she neared the spot where they'd fought. There was no sign of the psycho. Captain Matus still lay there, beside the street. And the coyote that had saved her life lay there too, a pool of congealing blood around its throat.

It must have been the animal she'd frightened when she went around that house. Amazing, that it would hide in the very bush into which she'd fallen. And then she remembered the distant howl she'd heard only moments before the animal exploded from cover and saved her. Could Hailey somehow be involved?

More important at the moment, was her attacker still nearby? He had seemed intent on doing her harm. But wouldn't he have chased her if that were the case? Had he been hurt enough to leave? Or did he know her well enough to understand she'd circle back because of Matus? She thought about calling for help. TPD might have a unit in the neighborhood. Only once they got her back in custody, she wasn't going to have a chance to help her uncle again before they caught or killed him

She took her time, because the psycho had told her Matus wasn't seriously injured and because he'd planned something much worse for her. But she went to the Sewa captain, all the same. And the psycho didn't spring out of the bushes or dash from behind a nearby building. Maybe the coyote had hurt him. Or maybe he'd only meant to scare her. If so, he'd succeeded.

Matus was still unconscious. His nose had stopped bleeding, though, and he was breathing normally. She tried shaking him a little and he moaned but didn't open his eyes.

"Captain," she whispered in his ear, pivoting her head from side to side, half expecting the psycho to launch himself out of the darkness at any moment. She shook Matus again. "We've got to get away from here," she told him.

He mumbled some kind of protest and she tried to get him to sit. He managed, woozily. His eyes blinked and he said something in a language that clearly wasn't English.

Heather checked around them again. Still nothing. From behind him, she got her arms under his and lifted. He wasn't a big man and she managed to get him to his feet.

"What's happening?" he said, then tried to fall down again.

She got herself under one of his shoulders and began walking him toward her car. Something painful gouged her from just under his coat. She felt good when she discovered it was a gun. It made her a little more confident about her prospects if they encountered the psycho again. She racked a round into the chamber and stuffed it in the waistband of her jeans.

Matus was getting a little steadier, though no less confused. She guided him down the center of the street, far enough from hiding places that she thought she could get to the gun before anyone got to them. It went well until she found her car and the two flat tires. He'd been there. And he'd probably be back. But Matus had followed her, too. She went through his pockets and found keys to a Toyota. Probably his own car, instead of a tribal vehicle. She punched the lock button and something chirped around the corner. She wasn't stuck here after all.

"Come on Captain. I'm thinking you should visit an emergency room." There had been a hospital just a few blocks north of Ms. Jardine's neighborhood. A good one, she thought, because it was the University of Arizona's Medical Center.

◇◇◇

The sheriff lay sprawled on the floor. His ears rang and he couldn't see anything except the afterimage of the flash that had shattered the windows. Something dripped down his face—blood. He'd been nicked by flying glass. Not seriously, if his exploring hands were to be believed.

"Mrs. Kraus?" he shouted.

"I'm all right," she answered, "but what the hell was that?"

The sheriff explored the darkness with his hands, found a corner of his desk. He could pull himself up that way, but he was likely to be right back on the floor if he didn't find his walker. He picked up a fresh cut from the glass littering the floor. That convinced him to raise his arms as he searched and, fortunately, the walker was right where he remembered leaving it—on the other side of his chair.

"Grenade, maybe, like at Mad Dog's." He used the desk and the walker to get to his feet, oriented himself with the desk, and started toward the nearest window. The blast hadn't blinded him. It had just knocked the lights out. Moonlight glowed on the other side of those windows. And something else flickered and burned out there.

"Lord God!" Mrs. Kraus was at the window ahead of him. "Would you look at that?"

And, finally, he could. Flames danced on the courthouse lawn. Some of them moved, scurrying this way and that in a manner that reminded him of the very different rules of the universe inside War of Worldcraft. This wasn't possible, was it? Fire didn't run around in circles. And then he understood. Fire didn't, but burning people did.

"That's a human being." He turned to Mrs. Kraus and told her to get the fire extinguisher. It was on the wall near the door to his office, an old-fashioned thing that would be heavy and unwieldy for her. But her spine wasn't still recovering from the bullet fragment that might cripple him for life.

"Lord God!" she said again, but he dimly saw her scramble across the room, grab the thing off the wall and disappear into the courthouse foyer. He followed as fast as he could. By the time he reached the front doors, the fire had stopped moving. It lay on the ground in the middle of the lawn while Mrs. Kraus directed a stream from the nozzle of the fire extinguisher and gradually dimmed its glow.

The smell was overpowering—burned meat. The sheriff knelt beside the smoldering figure and tried to find a pulse. Scorched flesh pasted itself to his hand and blistered his fingers. There was no pulse to be found.

"I may turn vegetarian," Mrs. Kraus gagged. "Who is it?"

The sheriff shook his head. There would be no way to identify this corpse in the traditional fashion. It was burnt and blasted beyond recognition.

"Ed Miller, maybe," he said. "At least that's his pickup, across the street at the edge of the park.

"You want me to call Doc Jones?"

Doc was the coroner, and the only MD who currently lived in Buffalo Springs. But the sheriff thought it wouldn't be necessary. Lights were coming on in nearly every house the sheriff could see. And people streamed out of those houses, pointing flashlights toward the courthouse.

"I'm guessing you won't have to. Looks like the blast woke everyone in Benteen County."

His cell chirped and he pulled it out of a pocket and told it who he was.

"I haven't found Mad Dog," Heather said, "but I may have met that killer of his."

Jesus! The blast and this body had driven Fig Zit's threat right out of his head. It was way too late to ask, but he did anyway.

"Are you all right?"

It was what the crowd arriving at the courthouse wanted to know of him and Mrs. Kraus. And in both Buffalo Springs and Tucson, "yes" was far too simple an answer.

◇◇◇

Emergency room personnel separated Mad Dog from the girl in short order. That didn't surprise him, really, since she was the one having the baby. But the way they did it made him think they suspected he'd abused her. She did have that bump on her head. And her nails had drawn blood when she squeezed his hand. To say nothing of the smudges of black paint on his skin here and there. They resembled bruising. His solid black left hand, the one she hadn't gotten to yet, just looked weird until they let him use a restroom and wash it and the rest of the paint off at last.

Mad Dog thought it might be time to leave. There were a couple of cops there with a shooting victim and he had the feeling the hospital people had asked them to talk to him when they got a moment. But he didn't quite make it to the exit before someone in scrubs intercepted him.

"Mr. Maddox," the man said, "your wife wants you with her for the delivery."

Mad Dog had had enough trouble with people accepting his IDs, checks and credit cards, that he'd kept one card in his original name, Harvey Edward Maddox. That was what he'd given them when they asked what insurance the young lady had. The young lady didn't have insurance. Mad Dog knew that. And when he'd said they should charge his card, they'd suddenly begun to treat him less like vermin.

"My wife?"

"Or whatever your relationship may be. And we'd like your help filling out some forms. The lady made it very clear she'd like you to be with her. Other than that, we can't seem to get much out of her."

The man opened a door that led back to the treatment rooms. Mad Dog glanced over his shoulder and saw that one of the cops had moved near the exit. Mad Dog followed the nurse, doctor, or whatever he was, and felt much better when the door swung shut behind them.

"Can you tell me Esperanza's date of birth?" the man said, ushering Mad Dog past a couple of gurneys, one occupied by someone quietly moaning an old Bob Dylan song instead of the prayer Mad Dog had expected.

"Esperanza?" Was that the girl's name? Mad Dog realized they hadn't gotten around to introductions.

"The woman you brought in, Mr. Maddox." The man gave him a funny look.

"Esperanza means Hope," Mad Dog said, improvising. He didn't want the hospital people to start thinking about involving the police again. "I usually call her Hope." This was the first time he'd associated any name with her, so he supposed "usually" qualified. "And, you know, some people don't think it's polite to ask a woman's age."

The guy in the scrubs continued to give Mad Dog a peculiar look, but it was a different kind of peculiar now.

"I see. How about blood type, allergies, medical conditions, anything that could help us with the treatment we provide?"

"We Cheyenne mostly stick to traditional medicine."

The man stopped in the middle of a hallway. "You don't really know this woman at all, do you? What are you, the coyote who smuggled her in?"

Two men passed a cross-hall, well down the corridor. Another figure in scrubs led a small, trim man cradling his left hand with his right. The guy with the injury didn't have braids or a beaded head band, nor was he wearing silver and turquoise jewelry. Nothing about him looked faintly Native American, but Mad Dog recognized him instantly—Fig Zit. Or, if not the character from the game, then the man who'd started the night's insanity when he knifed a Sewa Tribal Policeman a few hours ago.

"Answer me. Are you her coyote?"

"No coyote. Right now I'm Madwulf, and you'll have to excuse me. I've got a demon to exorcise."

◇◇◇

Heather pulled Matus' 4Runner into a lot across from the emergency room entrance. The captain had done a lot of recovering on the drive to the hospital. She opened a door and he reached over and put a hand on her arm before she could get out.

"I'm not going in there," he said.

"Why not? You're here, already. You don't know exactly what he did to you."

"I don't even know who did something to me. I was running beside the street and then you were helping me back to my car. Everything in between is a blank."

"That sounds like a good reason to see a doctor," she said, but she didn't pull away from him or climb out of the SUV.

"It could have been you that knocked me out," he said, "except you were ahead of me, not behind. I do remember that."

"So…?"

"So close the door and tell me why I shouldn't arrest you and turn you back over to TPD."

She pulled it shut. "Well, I went back for you and brought you here."

"There's that," he admitted. "But your uncle still killed my officer. I've got to bring him in, but it doesn't have to be dead.

Take me to him, persuade him to give himself up. I promise you he'll get his day in court."

"I don't know where he is," she said. "Besides, who do you think knocked you out back there? That wasn't Uncle Mad Dog. If it had been, and I was trying to help him get away with murder, he and I would be a long way from here right now."

He nodded, thinking about it.

"I think the man who took you out and attacked me was the guy who killed your officer. He looked a lot different than the way he was described at the ceremony, but I'll bet it was the same guy. This one knew my name and he had another switchblade he told me he'd use to do some elaborate carving. That fits with him knowing Mad Dog would be at Pascua. It fits with him setting up a murder and then framing my uncle."

"Yeah," he said. "Maybe. But it's a hell of a stretch. Your uncle's a thousand miles from home and hardly anybody knew you invited him to come here. What you're proposing requires someone not only know that, but go to the trouble of setting up a kill, and then not even killing his target, just framing him for the job. It's going to take one fine lawyer to sell that to a jury."

"Normally," Heather said. "But someone blew up Mad Dog's house in Kansas. And just now, someone tried to do the same to my father and his office. Your jury isn't going to buy all that as coincidence. There's your reasonable doubt."

Matus shook his head. "It's just so bizarre."

"But even you, you're starting to have doubts, aren't you?"

A siren had been getting louder and louder as they talked. Suddenly, it was deafening as the emergency vehicle appeared on the street behind them. Its lights strobed, turning cars and buildings and bushes alternating shades of red and white and blue. Heather watched the vehicle swing around to the side of the building.

"Oh my God!" she said. "That's him."

Matus didn't understand. "That's who? You talking about the ambulance?"

"No. Along the side of the hospital. I just saw him in their headlights."

"I can't see anyone," Matus said.

"There," Heather pointed. "The little guy holding his arm. That's the man who knocked you out and tried to hurt me. That's your killer."

Matus still couldn't see him. "Where?"

And then a door opened and a man in scrubs ushered a smaller man into the hospital.

"Quick!" Matus threw his door open and stumbled into the parking lot.

Heather was right behind him. Ahead, actually, since it took Matus a moment to regain his balance. She sprinted for the door, grabbed the handle, and yanked.

"Locked," she said. "How do we get in?"

Matus was reaching for his belt. "Damn," he said. "Bastard stole my gun."

Heather felt herself blush. At least it was too dark for him to notice. She pulled the gun from under her jacket and put it in his hands. "Sorry. I borrowed it while you weren't at your best. In case he came back."

He slammed the butt against the door, three times. "This is how we get in," he said. "This and my badge."

"Careful. I put a round in the chamber."

"Good," Matus said. "Because if someone doesn't answer this door in about thirty seconds, I'm going to blow a hole in the lock."

Heather didn't think shooting at a hospital was a good idea. She started to say so but then the door opened and Uncle Mad Dog was standing there.

She watched Matus' jaw drop as Mad Dog said, "Somehow I knew that was you. Hurry, I'll show you where Fig Zit went."

◇◇◇

Sheriff English removed his jacket and draped it over the charred ruin of what had once been a face. It would be too easily visible to the small crowd that had gathered in front of the courthouse. The distant street and porch lights weren't enough to illuminate the scene, but a gibbous moon was. That and the flashlight beams that were beginning to duel like low-wattage light sabers over the lawn and the seared body. The explosion had taken down the power and phone lines to the courthouse. The former arced and sputtered like an electric serpent, writhing at the south end of the building. The row of streetlights that should have lit the front of the courthouse was entering its third year of waiting for someone to get around to that county repair order.

The sheriff used his walker to steady himself as he went to one knee and felt for a billfold. Its leather was blackened and steaming. The driver's license had begun to weld itself to a credit card, but the picture and identity on its face were still recognizable. Not that there would be any matching this picture with this face. Both, however, apparently belonged to the Edward Miller whose pickup waited on the edge of Veterans' Memorial Park across the way.

"You all keep back now," Mrs. Kraus told the curious crowd, "and stop bothering us with your questions. You know we can't reveal stuff in the middle of an active investigation."

An aging Buick station wagon eased around the corner and nosed through the crowd. Its color was obscured, even when the occasional flashlight swept across the caked mud and layers of dust that covered its paint. The sheriff remembered a time when it had shone, back when Doc Jones, Benteen County Coroner, first brought home his converted ambulance. Sadly, it had carried far more dead than injured. And the sheriff could tell Doc was realizing it was about to perform that unhappy task yet again as he parked and climbed from behind the wheel. Doc's perpetually glum face sagged into a still more forlorn expression. The sheriff pulled himself to his feet and went to meet the coroner.

"When that explosion woke me, I figured I was needed," Doc said. "Though I hoped it wasn't in my official capacity. What happened?"

"Mrs. Kraus and I were in the office. Then bang, and we're in the dark and the windows are all blown in and someone's running around the lawn, burning to death. Mad Dog's house got blown up earlier tonight. Luckily, Mad Dog is out of town."

And in a hell of a mess down in Tucson, the sheriff might have added. It was just too complicated to get into, though. "I'm guessing this is the same fellow who was responsible for that. And that it's Ed Miller, since that's his truck over there and our corpse was carrying his wallet and driver's license."

Doc's face made the transition from sad to puzzled. "Ed Miller?" he said. "Why on earth would Ed want to blow up you and Mrs. Kraus?"

If he knew that, the sheriff thought, he'd have something to go on and, maybe, a way to help Mad Dog and Heather in far off Tucson. Maybe even, some hint that could lead him to Fig Zit.

"I haven't got a clue, Doc."

"Bombing you and Mrs. Kraus doesn't make any sense," Doc said. "Though Mad Dog, I can kind of understand."

"Really?" The sheriff was surprised.

"Yeah. Ed told me he finally got himself a decent paying job. He just started with the people planning that ethanol outfit your brother's been trying to keep out of Benteen County."

◇◇◇

Heather wasn't surprised when Mad Dog didn't wait to see how she and Captain Matus reacted to Mad Dog's surprising announcement.

"Follow me," her uncle told them. He whirled and went pounding down the hall like a fullback into an off-tackle hole his linemen had just opened.

She was even more surprised that Matus didn't seem to consider shooting Mad Dog in the back. The much-smaller Sewa followed on Mad Dog's heels, gun out, badge up. Not that there were any people trying to impede their progress. Heather found herself trailing the pack, and tossing an apology to a terrified nurse trying to climb the wall rather than deal with any of the wild bunch invading her hospital.

"One of these doors along here," Mad Dog called over his shoulder. "They were going in just as you knocked." He reached out and tried a knob and it turned.

"This one, I think," Mad Dog said. And then, just before Heather got to it, "Oh yeah. This one for sure."

Matus stopped dead in the middle of the doorway and Heather nearly ran over him. Then she saw why. Mad Dog stood in front of a desk heaped with papers and photographs of smiling people. Two other men were in the room with him. They both wore scrubs. One sat on the floor with his back to the desk and a surprised look in already cloudy eyes that stared at the syringe protruding from his torso, angling up, just under the sternum. The other man was lying against the far wall and he seemed to be having a seizure. He thrashed about madly, clawing at his neck and making strangled noises even though no one was doing any strangling.

Mad Dog bent and rolled him over. Heather could see that the man's neck was red and bleeding. With the way he was tearing at his throat, she wasn't sure he hadn't made those wounds to his own flesh. But his eyes were bugged out and his face had gone unnaturally pale.

"What?" Matus said. Heather wanted to echo him.

"God he's fast," Mad Dog said. "Fig Zit already killed that one and he's crushed this guy's windpipe."

"Get a doctor," Matus said.

"No time." Mad Dog fumbled in his pocket and came out with a red pocket knife. It was the one she'd told Matus about earlier in the evening, back when he was busy trying to link Mad Dog to a switchblade.

"What are you doing?" Matus said.

"Saving his life," Mad Dog said. "I hope."

Mad Dog bent and pulled the man's arms away with one hand and plunged the blade of the miniature Swiss Army knife into the strangling man's throat. Matus started to swing his gun up but Heather put a hand on his arm so it couldn't find a target.

"Wait," she told the captain. He stopped resisting her because gushes of air flew in and out of the wound and spotted Mad Dog's face with blood and added bright speckles to the bold pattern of his plaid shirt. A wild, wet sucking sound accompanied them, but the man Mad Dog had just knifed stopped fighting so hard. Blood-wet air hissed in and out of his lungs and the blue tint in his face began to return to normal.

"Get help," Mad Dog said, reaching for the throat of the man leaning against the desk and seeking a pulse. "One of these guys still needs it."

Heather turned back into the empty hall. "Help!" she yelled. When she looked back she saw a small bottle on the desk next to a picture of the man with the needle in his chest accepting an oversized check from someone with a big cowboy hat and a false grin.

Mad Dog glanced at the bottle and said, "What's potassium chloride?"

"That's the last part of the chemical cocktail they use to execute people," Matus said. "The one that induces cardiac arrest."

"I think Fig Zit knew that. And I think he saw this label."

"These people tried to kill him?" Heather asked.

"Looks that way," Mad Dog said. "But they only made him angry."

Mad Dog started across the room. That's when Heather first noticed that the smock hanging on the room's other door was still swaying.

"Where do you think you're going?" Matus said.

"After Fig Zit," Mad Dog replied. "He's hurt. He came for help and almost got ambushed. He'll just be trying to get out of here now. Maybe I can catch him."

Mad Dog opened the door. Heather saw another corridor beyond. And thought she heard the faint echo of footsteps, of someone running. She started to elbow her way around Matus but he had his gun pointing at Mad Dog's back again.

"Wait," the captain said.

"For what?" Mad Dog answered, not slowing down or looking back.

"For…for me," Matus said, and sprinted to the door Mad Dog had just gone through.

Someone had to stay and get help. The guy on the floor was breathing all right, but he could still drown in his own blood, right here at the back of the emergency department of a major hospital if she left him.

"Damn!" she said. She turned back to the corridor they'd followed to get here and shouted for help again.

◇◇◇

Ed Miller's truck sat nose first to one of the evergreens that had begun taking over Veterans' Memorial Park after the last round of Dutch Elm disease. The sheriff approached the vehicle, warning the crowd to stay clear. He was sure the truck had been the source of the explosive device that left Miller's body a charred mess on the courthouse lawn.

The bed of the old Ford held a couple of rolls of heavily insulated wire and a few rusty tools. Nothing particularly dangerous. The cab was another matter. A box of 40 mm rounds for an M79 grenade launcher sat on the passenger's seat—one missing. Incendiaries, if the sheriff's memory of shapes and color codes was correct. They wouldn't be much use since the grenade launcher had been left on a barbed wire fence as Miller ran away from the house he'd destroyed a few hours earlier.

But Ed had been a resourceful handyman ever since he came home from Southeast Asia. Not successful, maybe, but known for making do with whatever came to hand. In this case, what came to Miller's hand might have been smuggled home from Vietnam along with that grenade launcher, that and scrounged from a surprising inventory.

Back in Nam they called them Bouncing Betties—anti-personnel mines that, when triggered, ignited a propellant sending them to a height of about a meter before the main charge exploded. That spread the mine's shrapnel farther and did more damage to anyone unlucky enough to be in the vicinity of the person who set one off. One of those mines was duct taped to a cheap, re-corked wine bottle. That wasn't wine in there, though. Down on the floorboards on the passenger's side were three containers and a funnel. One was a gas can. The other two he wouldn't have recognized without the labels, BENZENE, and POLYSTYRENE. The sheriff didn't remember the proportions, but those were the essentials you combined to make napalm. When Miller couldn't shoot ready-made explosives into buildings anymore, he must have decided to use the mine to set off a homemade replacement.

The sheriff turned back and looked across the street toward the front of the courthouse. It hadn't burned. Except for missing windows, it looked remarkably undamaged. With better light, the sheriff thought he'd find chips in the bricks where shrapnel fragments from the Bouncing Betty had torn into its facade. Miller must have thrown his improvised device at the sheriff's window. And the unwieldy package evidently missed, hit the brick wall, ignited the launching device, and propelled the weapon back the way it had come. When it exploded and set off the napalm, it must have been right on top of Miller. Maybe the man had even tried to catch it for a second try. Whatever, much of his chest had burned away as he turned himself into a human torch that still smoldered and smelled of scorched meat.

That was simple enough to reconstruct. Why Miller would go to such extremes to protect his new job was something else again. As was why another of those jury-rigged devices lay on Miller's front seat.

It sat atop a little notebook. The sheriff reached through the truck's open window, carefully avoided the mine's detonator, and extracted the book. He used a flashlight he'd commandeered to examine Miller's tight scrawl.

"2," it read, "MD home. 5:30, court. 5:35, E-man home."

The last line seemed to indicate the sheriff's house was the intended destination for this last device. English glanced at his watch—5:12. Miller had decided to hit the courthouse early. On his own? On someone's instructions? Fig Zit's, maybe?

There was one other item on the seat beside the explosives. A cell phone. Its record of calls might answer the sheriff's question. He made very sure it wasn't connected to any of those grenades or the duct-taped combo, then pulled it out of the cab. He went through the phone's options and was disappointed to find no numbers programmed into its memory. But there was another selection labeled "Recent." When the sheriff chose that, he got "Received" and "Dialed." The "Received" column was dominated by someone labeled "Private." "Dialed" went almost exclusively to "FI." He selected that one and punched the call button. The phone rang once before a man's voice screamed in the sheriff's ear.

"Idiot! Don't you check your messages? Didn't you hear me yelling at you not to do Mad Dog's place? And you weren't supposed to hit the courthouse until five-thirty."

The voice sounded faintly familiar, but cell phones never helped with voice recognition. The sheriff answered the tirade with a noncommittal grunt.

"Well, did you kill them at least?"

The sheriff grunted again.

"Wait," the voice said. "Who is this?"

The sheriff hit the disconnect button. Who could he find to tell him what number this thing had dialed? And, more important, show him where the phone it reached was located? The Kansas Highway Patrol would probably send a cruiser to pick the cell up and analyze numbers and addresses for him, but he wanted faster results. Before he could think about local possibilities, Miller's phone rang. Why not, the sheriff thought. He flipped it open and held it to his ear and made a noise that might have been "hello," his name, or even the static of a bad connection.

It was the same voice, the one that had just asked if he and Mrs. Kraus were dead. "Give me your security code."

The sheriff didn't have that so he just stood and listened. It didn't take long.

"Incompetents. I'm surrounded by incompetents. So I'm probably talking to you, Englishman. Well, maybe you won this round, but remember, your daughter should be experiencing the ultimate agony about now."

The phone went dead before the sheriff managed to get out the expletive he had in mind. He said it anyway, because that was all a crippled man half a country away from his endangered daughter could do.

◇◇◇

"How may I help you?"
The voice was the same, the professional thought, and yet not the same. This time, the man at Fick's was surprised by his call. And that meant...?

"How is my report on the girl coming?" He kept his lips close to the phone's receiver. He thought he'd shaken the people following him through the maze of halls in this hospital, but caution was how you survived in this business.

"Uh, you said sixty minutes...."

"I'm in a dynamic situation and my schedule has been altered. You wouldn't know anything about that, would you?"

"I...well...." The man at Fick's was rattled. And the professional thought he understood why. Fick's had betrayed him.

"You found my client, didn't you?"

"Why, no, of course not. We would have informed you...."

"And he made you a better offer, didn't he?" The professional jogged up a staircase to stay ahead of the hunters. Considering the fresh bodies he'd left behind, those pursuing him would soon number more than the ones he'd heard, pounding down that hall from the office where he'd left one dead and one dying.

"I don't know what you're...."

"Yes you do. Give me his name and location and I'll double whatever he paid you."

"No, really," the voice from Fick's said, in spite of its full bodied tone, sounding young and scared and tinged with beginning panic. "I don't understand what you're talking about. What's happened?"

"Oh, you know all right," the professional said as he let himself out onto a deserted corridor one floor up. "If you don't answer me now, understand that everyone at Fick's goes on my schedule, gratis."

"Is there a problem? Didn't the nurse meet you? Didn't…?"

"The client's name. Immediately, or start looking over your shoulder."

A pair of women in scrubs came out of a door behind him and he flowed around a corner. When he checked, they were going the other way, moving fast and conversing in business-like tones.

"Just a, uh…. Just a minute."

"Now!" the professional hissed.

"All right. We found your client. Your client is, uh…."

They were going to lie to him. He knew it. And the name they gave him confirmed it.

"…is uh, Pamela Epperson."

"That's interesting," he said, moving back down the corridor, looking for an exit. "Because, from what you've told me, Pamela Epperson couldn't pay more than a few thousand dollars, even if she borrowed to do it."

"We lied. The information we gave you about her. It was altered."

"You lied, all right. Because I didn't get the information about Mad Dog's girlfriend from you. I got it from another source."

"She may have gotten to them, too. She must have…."

But she couldn't, of course. She was just a kid, not that long out of school, trying to break into the big time by playing piano and singing in an off-the-strip bar in Vegas. He broke the connection and took a chance, pushing the button for an elevator.

He'd spoken to the client. His client sounded like a man, but voices could be altered and identities falsified. No one knew that better than the professional. Still, the client had access to huge sums of money. The professional's instincts, and additional research, told him Pam Epperson didn't have the finances or the contacts to pull this off. And no reason to want it done in the first place. The voice at Fick's had set him up, then grasped for a straw to convince him otherwise.

The elevator was empty. He took another chance and pushed the button that said lobby. And, when his phone began ringing on the way down, he turned it off without even looking to see who was calling.

The lobby was almost as empty as the hall he'd just left. A couple in one corner was deep in a discussion of life and death matters. A woman at a reception desk spoke on the phone as she consulted her computer. Another man dozed over yesterday's newspaper. There was a cell phone on the arm of the sleeping man's chair. The professional walked by as he headed toward the exit where, just outside, another couple stood smoking cigarettes and peering into the darkness for the reassurance they hadn't found inside. No one was paying attention to him. Just in case, though, the professional fumbled for his cell phone and dropped it onto the carpet near the dozing man's feet. He bent, picked it up, and deftly switched it with the one on the arm of the chair. It was the same make and a similar model. The switch might go undetected for some time. As he exited the building, he used the new phone to dial another of his research sources. One he hadn't used on this project. One he still trusted.

"Good morning," a voice said in his ear. "May we have your log-in code, please?"

He gave it, from memory, all twenty letters and numbers. And, when they asked what they could do for him, he said, "I want your maximum effort on this. As soon as it can be done, I want to know who is behind Fick's Internet Technology and where I can find them."

◇◇◇

Heather crouched among the ornamental bushes at the edge of a parking garage north of the emergency room. Her gut feeling told her the psycho's car was somewhere nearby. That he'd have to come back this way—that his escape would lead him past the spot where he'd been let into the hospital.

At first, she'd thought he must have somehow followed her to the University Medical Center, the way he'd somehow followed her to that lonely back street. But the psycho was hurt. And, even if he'd known she'd brought Matus here for treatment, he hadn't approached the building like a stalker. Her adversary had come here like a would-be patient with special connections. And then those special connections had turned on him and tried to kill him. Now, if she was right, the psycho was running. He'd probably go back for his car, which, since he'd come to the building from the north, was most likely in this parking garage or the neighborhood just beyond.

She shouldn't be going after him alone. She knew that. But it wasn't like Uncle Mad Dog and Captain Matus had given her a choice. They'd left her. Gone after him together. Maybe they'd gotten lucky and caught him and she'd just huddle in these bushes until the sun came up, or someone reported her suspicious behavior. Or she'd lurk here long enough to convince herself the psycho wasn't coming.

Getting out of the room with the dead doctor hadn't been hard. Once she resumed shouting, help came fast. After all, they were in the offices just behind the emergency department. And then, as soon as Uncle Mad Dog's patient was receiving real medical attention, she beat it. Went right back down that hall she'd entered by and out the door at the rear of the building. She hadn't paused to look back to see how things were going behind her because security forces and the police would be all over that office real quick. And once they got hold of her, she'd be off the street until this was over.

Heather checked her fanny pack, hoping a gun might have somehow gotten in there when she wasn't looking. No such luck, of course. She didn't even have her can of pepper spray. She must have left it in her purse. Her weapons were all in the pockets of her jeans—a miniature Swiss Army knife, pink handle and all, and two sets of keys. Her rental car's and the ones for Matus' 4Runner. And her badge. Not what she wanted to go up against a man who'd promised her such elaborate and twisted tortures a short time before. But he *was* hurt. He'd been holding one hand with the other when that guy in the scrubs led him into the hospital. And she'd held her own against him while he was still healthy. For a little while, at least. It made her feel better until she remembered that the psycho, while hurt, had just crushed one guy's larynx, killed another with a syringe, and gotten out of the room before she and Mad Dog and Matus, not that far behind, could get there.

And then none of that mattered because there he was, on the sidewalk that led from the hospital. He held his injured hand to his abdomen, as if even letting it hang and swing normally was seriously uncomfortable. His cell phone was in his good hand and to his ear. As he went by, he was issuing quiet orders to whoever was on the other end of that call.

"...everything you can get me that might link...."

The night breeze rustled the leaves of the bushes she was hiding behind and that was all she caught.

Now what? Maybe she should have tried to take him while they were close to the emergency room—where she might have attracted attention and gotten help if things didn't go well. But what-ifs and might-have-beens were useless now. She could go back for help and probably lose him, or....

She chose column B, slipping from behind the shrubbery and onto the sidewalk. He was walking fast, seemingly involved in his conversation and not concerned about being followed. She sprinted to the stairway at the end of the garage and ducked in there. When she peered out, he was entering the neighborhood. It was darker there. Not so many street lights.

He was good, she knew that. But maybe he was too good, or thought he was, and that would prove his fatal weakness. Maybe he was so certain he had gotten away and was clear that he didn't think he needed to check behind him. Maybe she really could take him. Or find out where he was going and call for help.

A brick wall separated the loop road around the hospital from the neighborhood. Heather made that her next stop. She crept to the corner and checked for him again. He was out of sight. He'd gone around a nearby street corner, but he wasn't far because she could still hear the low murmur of his end of the phone conversation. She picked some promising bushes and sprinted. He was about half a block down, opening the door of a generic Japanese rental car. The dome light didn't come on after he opened the door. This guy thought of everything.

What now? He had disappeared into the car but the driver's door was still open. If she could get there quickly and quietly enough, she'd come up on his left side—his bad hand. That, and being behind the wheel, would limit his ability to defend himself. She could probably kill him quickly enough—crush his throat the way he had for that man in the hospital, or drive his nose cartilage straight into his brain. But she wanted him alive. If only she had the pepper spray.

She crossed the street and began closing the distance between herself and that open door. She was a car length behind when she heard the unmistakable sound of a pistol's hammer being cocked. She turned and there he was, just on the other side of the car. His gun was centered on her chest. He'd known she was behind him all along.

"You're good," he said, echoing what she'd thought about him only a few minutes before, "but not as good as you think. That can get you in real trouble."

She was considering whether she should dive forward or backward, and where she might run that would minimize the chance of him hitting her with at least half a dozen opportunities. Her plans changed when he let the hammer back down and slipped the weapon in his belt.

"I was going to hurt you very badly," he said as casually as if they'd just sat down over triple espresso shakes at the neighborhood coffee house, "and I would have enjoyed it. But now, things have changed. I think we're on the same side."

"No way."

"Oh, yes. The client who hired me to hurt you, and frame your uncle, just put out a hit on me. That changes everything. Now, you and I need to cooperate, share information."

He couldn't have surprised her more if he'd broken into a soft-shoe routine. Actually, that would have made some sense because she was already convinced he was insane.

"But we can't do it here," he said, and she realized distant sirens were coming their way. "You found me. Unless I'm out of here soon, so will everyone else who's looking for me. So get in the car. Let's get out of here."

"Are you kidding?"

He shrugged and walked around to the driver's door. "Suit yourself. I don't have time to argue. I know quite a bit about what's happened to your uncle. What's still supposed to happen to him. And to you. I'll tell you what I know and maybe you can tell me who might want it done. Then, when we understand who we're after, we can see about putting an end to it. Separately, of course. And each in our own fashion."

He closed the door and started the car. "Sit in the back if you feel safer there," he said. "And feel free to bring the wolf."

Hailey bounded from behind a bird of paradise plant on the dark lawn near where the psycho had been standing. She nuzzled Heather's hand and then walked over and put claw marks on the rental car's back door.

Damn, Heather thought. In all those self-defense classes, the first thing they told you was never get in the car with the bad guy. Of course, they hadn't mentioned what to do if you could take a wolf along for support. There was only one way to find out. She opened the door and followed Hailey into the demon's lair.

◇◇◇

English decided to set up a temporary sheriff's department in Doc Jones' section of the Buffalo Springs Medical Clinic. The choice was easy. Doc had two phone lines, cable for his computer, and he'd offered the keys to his place before transporting Miller's charred body from the courthouse yard to Klausen's Funeral Home where he would do the autopsy.

The sheriff had disarmed Miller's homemade bomb. He'd learned how to do that with Bouncing Betties while he was in the service. Then he took all the explosives out of the truck and locked them in his office safe. Mrs. Kraus gathered notebooks, telephone numbers, and her CDs for War of Worldcraft.

"Install that on Doc's computer and log in as soon as you can," the sheriff said as he sent her out the door. "Fig Zit may put in another appearance. And check with that Worldcraft technician. He may have the list of accounts in our area by now."

"Would that be before or after I contact the telephone company to get our calls forwarded to Doc's office?" Mrs. Kraus grumbled as she headed for her car. The sheriff didn't pay any attention because he was busy answering his cell phone. The incoming call had a Tucson area code so he took the call immediately.

"Parker, here," a familiar voice said.

"Any word?"

"Oh heck!" someone said, poking their head into the sheriff's office. "This is gonna bust your budget."

The sheriff turned to tell them to get out, that this was a crime scene. But it was Supervisor Macklin. Since Macklin was personally responsible for the budget cuts that prevented the county from having even one round-the-clock deputy anymore, the sheriff was inclined to tell him to get out anyway, but he didn't.

"No. No word," Parker said, refocusing him on the phone. "I was hoping you'd heard something. Things aren't going great. We've got nothing on your brother or Heather yet."

"Really?" English was surprised, but not exactly disappointed. For some reason, he decided not to pass along what Heather had been through, or where. "I thought, with that APB your assistant chief put out on Mad Dog...."

"You heard about that, huh? I wasn't going to say anything."

"Yeah, I know," the sheriff said. "Bastard told me about it himself."

"Watch your language, Sheriff," Supervisor Macklin said. Not only was the man a political pain in the neck, he oozed holier-than-thou attitude. The sheriff would have popped the guy in the nose a couple of years ago if it weren't for his situation—losing his wife to cancer and bringing up two boys on his own. It was too much like what English had gone through.

Sergeant Parker said, "I would have gone to the chief to get that order rescinded, but he's out of town and unavailable. I don't like the way this is shaping up."

This wasn't the time for the sheriff to learn about the politics in Tucson's police department.

"Last I heard from Fig Zit was a threat to harm Heather." Parker didn't know about Fig Zit or War of Worldcraft and the sheriff had to take a few moments to bring her up to speed.

Then she said, "Hang on." And didn't wait for him to agree. Parker just put him on hold for a frustrating minute.

Supervisor Macklin chose to fill the silence. "That crazy brother of yours deserves whatever he gets. And your snooty daughter...."

Parker came back on the phone before the sheriff could react. "I just got word of a murder at a local emergency room. And a second attempt. A doctor and a nurse. Not your family."

The sheriff hadn't realized he was holding his breath until he released it.

"I'm on my way there," Parker continued, "because two of the suspects are described as a big bald guy and a pretty young woman with a badge. I'll keep you posted."

The sheriff started to beg her to ask the responding units to go easy on those two, but the phone was already dead in his hand. Parker really was on her way. He tried Heather's cell and got her voice mail. Her phone was off.

"Shit!" the sheriff muttered, clicking the phone closed and feeling, yet again, utterly helpless in the face of this distant emergency.

"Really, Sheriff. I'll thank you to watch your mouth," Macklin scolded him.

That was it, the sheriff's last straw. His camel collapsed.

The sheriff maneuvered his walker toward the door. When he was face to face with Macklin, he stopped. "Yes, sir, I should probably do that. But in the meantime why don't you fuck off?"

◇◇◇

"Wow! It's a boy." Mad Dog said.

"Works out that way, about half the time," the obstetrician said, holding the infant up so Esperanza could see him. The no-longer-pregnant but just-as-illegal alien reached for her son and took him in her arms. She looked at Mad Dog and said, "Thank you for coming back."

Mad Dog hadn't intended to. Not that he'd wanted to abandon her, but he'd been hot on the heels of Fig Zit. Well, for a little while at least. And then he'd been sure Fig Zit had gone up a stairwell while Matus was sure the killer had gone down. When the door at the top was locked, Mad Dog went up another level and got thoroughly lost until he found himself face to face with one of the people who'd checked Esperanza into the hospital in the first place.

"Come on," the nurse had said. "She needs you now."

And Mad Dog had gone and held her hand. Now he wondered if he should maybe get it x-rayed in case Esperanza had actually fractured every bone below his wrist.

"That hurt pretty bad, huh?" Mad Dog said.

The obstetrician rolled her eyes and the nurse said, "Oh no. I think she kept screaming like that because she was glad to see you."

"I was glad to see you," Esperanza told him. "You may not think so, but having a good man like you, and a shaman to boot, it helped me a lot."

Mad Dog shuffled his feet and beamed, and neither the obstetrician nor the nurse made another wisecrack.

"I hope you're not mad at me," Esperanza said, "sneaking in so my baby can be a citizen. I just want him to be part of this great nation."

Mad Dog was too psyched by the miracle of birth to consider immigration issues. "Course not," he said.

A different nurse stuck his head into the delivery room. "Doctor, I need your attention out here for a minute."

"Congratulations to all of you," the doctor said, and smiled and left the delivery room.

"I'd like to name him after you," Esperanza said. "But Mad Dog, that's kind of a tough name for such a little one to carry. You got any others?"

"I was christened Harvey Edward Maddox."

"Xavier," Esperanza said. "I like that. I'll tell him he's actually *Perro Loco* when he's old enough."

"Gosh," Mad Dog said, overwhelmed.

The door opened and the male attendant reappeared, summoning their nurse. The man pushed a chair over beside the bed and suggested Mad Dog sit in it. "I bet you'd like to hold the baby."

Mad Dog started to sit but Esperanza said, "No. You got to go now, Xavier Eduardo. Can't you see, they're trying to keep you occupied. I think *la policia*, maybe, will be here in a few minutes. Besides, don't you have a demon to catch?"

"Uh, no, really," the attendant said, but he backed toward the door, looking nervous, then ducked out as if Mad Dog were likely to do him serious harm.

"Thanks," Mad Dog told her. He opened the door and discovered all the delivery room people had disappeared. "Looks like you're right. I better go."

An elevator across the hall showed ascending numbers and Mad Dog thought he'd catch it back to the lobby level.

"Hurry," Esperanza called. "I got a feeling they're almost here. Run, *Señor* Mad Dog. Run like the wolf."

It was funny she put it that way, he thought, but the elevator opened on a pair of uniformed security guards and there was no time to ask her about it. There was only time to do exactly what she'd suggested. He ran like the wolf.

◇◇◇

Heather had ridden too far in silence. Hers was because she'd been trying to decide whether to open the door and make a break for it every time the psycho's car slowed or stopped at an intersection. His, she guessed, because he was trying to decide how much he wanted to say and how he wanted to say it.

"Where are we going?" Heather said, looking over Hailey's shoulder to read a street sign. They were headed east on Fort Lowell Road. They'd come quite a distance from the university and were in an area of mixed townhomes and horse properties, and not a single living human being as far as her eye could see.

"Anywhere, nowhere," he answered. "Just driving, since I can't think of a good place for a professional assassin, a deputy sheriff, and a wolf to sit down for a chat in the wee hours of the morning. Unless you have a suggestion?"

"No, I'm just a tourist."

They turned right at what might be a good spot for tourism. A bronze bugler, some old adobe buildings, and a sign indicated that they were at Fort Lowell and that it might have once been a cavalry post.

"Okay. Then be quiet and listen. You want to save your uncle, and your family, and yourself. I want to ensure my own safety. To do that, we have to locate some people. You're more likely to know who they are than I am, but you're not going to be open with me until you understand what's at stake."

And not then, either, Heather thought as they followed the street south. Two other cars occupied this wide stretch of asphalt, though neither within half a mile.

"You probably think of me as some kind of psychopath, perhaps a serial killer."

He was perceptive, at least, Heather thought.

"You would do well to revise that. I enjoy my work, a great deal. But I'm a quintessential businessman. I simply happen to trade in death and terror. My principal interest in doing to you the things I described earlier this evening was financial. I was told to injure you, to humiliate you, in those very specific fashions. Your mutilation was worth $78,000 to me, my dear. Someone who knows you and your family offered to pay that much to have you scarred for life. And he was in a hurry to have it done. I want you to consider who might hate you that much. And who could afford it, as well as the $120,000 I received to establish your uncle as the prime suspect in the murder of a member of the Sewa tribal police. Then, the $240,000 I was offered to scare a cop and make sure your uncle isn't captured alive."

That let out everyone Heather knew. Well, maybe it didn't. Plenty of farmers in Benteen County paid prices like that for land or the machinery to farm it. But they were cash poor. Rich in ground and tractors, maybe, but without much money on hand. The rest were absentee landlords, corporations that were wealthy enough, perhaps, but with managers who had never met her, or even set foot in Benteen County. Besides, she couldn't think of anyone who hated her like that. She had a few casual enemies, she supposed, but $78,000?

"Don't focus on yourself," he said. "You're incidental. Just a tool to hurt or manipulate someone else—your father, I presume. But all this started with your uncle. Consider him first."

Uncle Mad Dog? He seemed to specialize in doing stuff that outraged most of Benteen County. Dad said he'd been an odd-ball almost forever. Well, at least after his football career ended with a blown knee and a lost college scholarship. When he'd come back to Benteen County, he was a hippie. One of those long-haired, peacenik freaks who outraged conservative rural communities like Buffalo Springs during the Vietnam War. Her dad had explained it was like Uncle Mad Dog to enjoy annoy-ing people, especially when doing so made them think outside their comfort zones.

Mad Dog had organized himself into the local Black Power movement, boycotted grapes, studied and practiced several Eastern philosophies, and then, decided he was a natural-born Cheyenne Shaman. That, at least, he'd stuck with. But along the way he'd angered, or worse, virtually everyone in the county. He'd passed petitions demanding the impeachment or resignation of almost every president. In rural Kansas, Bill Clinton was the only one she could remember him having much success with. He'd started a wolf-hybrid rescue effort that infuriated every cattle and sheep rancher she knew. Worse, he'd screwed up the wind farm project that was going to make the community rich. And if that wasn't enough, he'd been trying to convince people the new ethanol plant would do them more harm than good…and he'd actually convinced some folks it would cause irreparable damage to the Ogallala Aquifer. But still, hiring this psycho to assassinate Mad Dog or hurt her made no sense.

"My uncle has some enemies, but no one who would throw away that kind of money when they could just pay him a visit with a deer rifle and take him out for the price of a single cartridge. And why here in Tucson? Uncle Mad Dog wasn't even planning to come until the last minute."

"Let me tell you about my visit to Tucson," the psycho said. "I flew in last night with a contract. I was hired to pay a visit to a local government employee. The person in question had done favors for some local special interests, but he was coming under suspicion and considering going public to save his own skin. I was brought in to demonstrate that it wasn't just his skin that was at risk. I spent the night in a hotel near the airport and applied some incentives to remain silent during the target's lunch break. I didn't kill him, I presume, because that could blow the case wide open. Then I got a call from my client asking if I'd be interested in a second job while I was in town. Double the money and it was all being set up for me. I would pass myself off as a visiting dignitary to the Yaqui Easter ceremonies—a representative of a distant Indian tribe. A package was delivered with all sorts of helpful documentation for the identity I would assume. It also contained photos and background information on my new target and your uncle—and a knife of the sort I favor that had your uncle's name etched on the handle.

"On Friday? All this was delivered to you on Friday? Even I didn't know Uncle Mad Dog was coming until he got here."

"Someone knew. Or was reasonably sure."

"How?"

"I don't know," the psycho said. "Maybe they hacked into his emails. Maybe he's got some kind of GPS device on his car. You'd be surprised how easy it is to track someone these days.

And he did come, right where I'd been told he'd be. So I did my job and was about to catch a flight out of town when things began going wrong. I got another call from the same client. I got that call after disposing of the cell phone I used to stay in touch with him. I got it on a new, sterile phone that the client shouldn't have known about, let alone been able to reach. And I was offered $240,000 to convince a local cop that your uncle might be dangerous, then ensure that Tucson police don't take him alive. At that point, the price for my activities here was $420,000. And that was before you were added to the mix, along with the indication I might earn several more fees for later work in Kansas and Las Vegas."

"Kansas? Las Vegas? Then they must want to hurt Dad. And Pam Epperson, Uncle Mad Dog's girlfriend," Heather said.

"It does seem that each job was intended to get at people who know your uncle. People who mean something to him. And we're talking about serious money, here. I had the impression there would be more than one target in Kansas. My fees would have been well over half a million. But, perhaps my client decided to cut his expenses. My off-shore account had received $300,000 by then. Doing you and your uncle would have brought in another $198,000. But then our first meeting was interrupted by that coyote."

He was favoring his left hand, she noticed, but using it on the steering wheel. The coyote hadn't crippled him.

They had turned again, a few blocks back, onto another wide, empty thoroughfare. Heather had been so focused on the man who once planned to mutilate her and kill her uncle that she no longer had the foggiest idea where they were. Hailey seemed more interested in the city than the psycho, but Heather was damn glad to have her along.

"People in my line of work require support—firms that make us reservations, rent cars, and provide research. Generally, these aren't firms you can find in the yellow pages or by Googling the web. We get them by word of mouth, through secure internet chat rooms, and by testing what they're willing to do for us. Not long ago I began using a group that calls itself Fick's Internet Technologies. I have to wait for them, sometimes, but they're the best I've ever used. Does the name mean anything to you?"

"Fick? No," she said. "Nothing."

"After the coyote, I called them. They arranged treatment for me—private, unnoticed treatment. But, apparently, they arranged something more."

"I know," Heather said. "We were right behind you. I saw what was in that syringe."

"So I assume," he continued, "that the client I've been dealing with regarding you and your family decided to replace me. Or that I wasn't needed anymore and money could be saved."

"But wouldn't that mean they'd have to pay the doctor and the nurse?" Heather asked.

"Perhaps not. As quickly as Fick's managed to set that up, those people may have already been available."

"Killer doctors on call?" Heather couldn't imagine it.

"Not professionals like me. Not the way you're thinking. But, maybe, part of the special interest group that brought me here in the first place. People who knew why I was here and what I am. Can you grasp that?"

"Sure. But what would these people have to do with Uncle Mad Dog?"

"Ah, there's the question." He slowed for a stoplight, though there were no other cars visible on the wide rivers of asphalt. A well-lit sign proclaimed they were at Swan and Twenty-Second. "Some kind of relationship exists between a massively wealthy special interest group here and your uncle. Most of my research on him was done by Fick's so I'm not sure it's accurate, but I understand he's been opposing an ethanol plant in your hometown?"

"Yes. That's true. He says it causes more pollution to create ethanol than to just use petroleum. But he's begun converting people based on all the water that will be pumped from our aquifer, and the…."

"Who? Who's behind your ethanol plant?"

"I don't know," Heather said. "Outside investors, mostly. Supervisor Macklin heads the local group, though I think nearly all our board of supervisors are part of it."

"Names," he demanded. "I need their names."

A warning growl gurgled out of Hailey's throat but Heather began giving them to him anyway.

The psycho slammed on the brakes, nearly spilling Heather to the floor boards. Hailey, somehow, had set herself, as if she expected it. But she stood just behind the psycho, teeth bared, as thoroughly and regally un-amused as a princess with a pea under her mattress.

"There," he pointed out the windshield. "See that bill-board?"

It was a huge sign. The owner's name and smiling cowboy-hat topped countenance dwarfed the names of housing developments he offered, restaurants he owned, and makes of automobiles he sold. It was a familiar face, though. She'd seen it on that dead doctor's desk at the University Medical Center.

He pointed at the sign. "Does your Supervisor Macklin have a wealthy Arizona relative named Bobby Earl?"

Now that she thought about it, she remembered hearing something like that.

"Yeah," she said. "Billy Macklin, the supervisor's son was bragging to someone in a booth behind me at our local café last fall. I thought it was all hype about the ethanol plant. But Billy said he'd arranged for an Arizona cousin to finance a business Billy would run."

"Get out," the psycho said. He had filled his good hand with the gun again.

"What?"

"Get out. You and the wolf. Now. I've got what I need from you. And you've got what you need from me. Use it."

She supposed he was right, except that she was miles from her car, or Matus', for that matter.

She opened the door and Hailey waited until Heather was safely on the sidewalk before joining her.

"What are you going to do?" Heather didn't expect an answer, but she got one.

"I'm going to ask my original target who he was working for. If Bobby Earl Macklin's name comes up, I'll be paying him a visit. Then, when I've cleaned up that part of the mess, I'll go after Fick."

He popped the clutch and that slammed her back door closed. She watched, for a moment, as his tail lights faded into the distance. She turned to see if Hailey had any suggestions about where they should start. The wolf had disappeared.

◇◇◇

Mad Dog ran toward downtown. Not because that was where he'd been headed before, but because that was where the nearest hospital exit pointed him. And it didn't hurt that he found cover in the form of outbuildings, trees, and bushes that screened him from whoever might be following. He ran fast and easy, because he'd been running practically every day of his life and, in spite of his age, his joints seemed to thrive on it.

He was near the university. Esperanza had said the University Medical Center was just north of the main campus. But even without that knowledge, he would have known. The homes here were obviously rentals—lots more cars than any residential area should expect, and an unusually high percentage of sporty ones. He spotted Greek letters in front of a couple of large houses. He heard the thump of base from a stereo, in spite of the unholy hour. And then he heard the voices—not loud, but angry.

"…call the cops," someone said. The words should have had Mad Dog taking the first turn away, but the response made it impossible.

"Not before I blow you to hell."

The second voice was male. The first had been in a tenor range that left gender uncertain. Mad Dog slowed, slipped between a sleek Porsche and a boxy Scion and onto the sidewalk.

The first voice was speaking again. Soft, pleading. He couldn't make out most of the words but decided this one was female.

"Not afraid…off the drugs…gun down.…"

A thick privet hedge separated the yard where the voices were from the sidewalk along which Mad Dog approached. He slowed and paused at the corner to peer around the neatly groomed leaves.

A couple stood on a large porch—one with several chairs and a glider. The man was about six feet tall and wiry. She wasn't much smaller, but the hand he had wrapped in her hair and the chrome-plated revolver he held to her temple put her at a noticeable disadvantage. The base note boomed out the open door behind them from somewhere inside the house.

Englishman had often complained that the only duty calls he truly dreaded answering were domestic violence cases. And that's what this was, whether they were college students or faculty members, lovers or a wed-until-death-did-them-part pair. If the guy was on drugs, the until-death thing might not be far away.

"Cheating bitch," the man hissed, yanking her hair with each syllable. She stumbled and her head hit one of the plastered pillars that flanked the front steps. Hard enough to hurt, Mad Dog was sure, though she didn't cry out. The pistol stuck with her and the change of angle allowed Mad Dog to see that the guy's face was twisted with rage. The light from one of the windows was enough to reveal a little spittle running out of the corner of the guy's mouth. He wore only a pair of shorts. She had on an oversized t-shirt and a pair of jeans. A backpack lay at her feet. She was leaving him but he'd stopped her, Mad Dog guessed.

"Let me go," she said. "Come on. We can talk about this in the morning."

"You won't see morning," he said. He banged her head against the pillar with each word and Mad Dog could see that the pistol was cocked.

Shit, he thought. But he smiled like some evangelical door-to-door vacuum cleaner salesmen as he stepped around the hedge and started walking toward the house. "Hey," he called. "It's a boy. I wanted you to be the first to know, buddy."

The rage on the guy's face didn't quite disappear, but it took on a hint of puzzlement. The girl swung her eyes, since she couldn't turn her head, and caught sight of Mad Dog advancing across the yard. If anything, she seemed more afraid of him than the guy with the pistol.

"He's got dark eyes," Mad Dog said. "Cute little nose." Mad Dog ran a hand across his shaved head and added, "And his mother's hair, thank goodness."

"Who…?" the guy with the gun started to ask, but at least the gun had swung away from her temple. The man behind it was no longer sure which of them to target.

As he neared the porch, Mad Dog reached for his pocket and said, "Here, have a cigar." He didn't have any cigars, of course, but he fished around in his jeans and then pulled his hand out as if it held something precious. The man's eyes followed and Mad Dog snapped out his other hand and snatched the gun from the guy's grasp. He used the hand that was supposed to have had a cigar to punch the man's throat. Sudden breathing difficulties forced Mad Dog's "buddy" to let go of the woman's hair.

"There," Mad Dog said. "Now isn't that better?"

Which came under the heading of counting your chickens before you even build the coop, since the girl came at Mad Dog, swinging and shrieking.

Luckily, the guy who'd been about to blow her brains all over the front yard just stood there with his jaw open in confusion and the effort to get his breath back. And that, of course, was the moment when the police cruiser pulled up out front and hit them with its spotlight—and another welcome-to-Tucson moment for Mad Dog.

◇◇◇

The sheriff jotted notes as he talked to the technician at War of Worldcraft. In the background, Mrs. Kraus argued with someone at the phone company about switching the sheriff's calls to the clinic while she loaded her copy of the game on Doc's computer.

"Eight clients in your zip code," the tech was saying. "I'd start with this nut who signed up under the name Mad Dog."

"Right." The sheriff decided it would take too long to explain about that. "I know him. Who are the others?"

"Well, you already know Mrs. Kraus, of course. The rest are Kevin Peirce, Frank Ball, Isaac Miller, Dana Miller, Cole Macklin, and—a relative, maybe—Billy Macklin."

The sheriff knew them all, though mostly not well. He'd just succeeded in insulting Billy's and Cole's supervisor father. Isaac Miller was a nephew of the corpse Doc was working on. Dana, his big sister, had been Billy's date tonight. Suddenly, the sheriff wanted to know, real bad, what Billy and Dana had been doing out by Mad Dog's place when it blew up.

The Miller kids' father was a partner in Ed's repair business. Kevin Peirce and Frank Ball were high-school age, like Isaac and Cole. Juniors or sophomores, the sheriff thought. None of them were part of the wild bunch—the local jocks, or the wilder would-be cowboys. Instead, they were serious students, nerds…. Computer nerds, maybe? And what was it the Millers called their repair business? Oh yeah, WE CAN FIX IT.

And the light went on in that little bubble above the sheriff's head. He had it. Fix it—Fig Zit. But what did a computer game have to do with a local repair service? Something, evidently. Two bombings, and a planned third, seemed to be tied to it.

"You need addresses?"

The sheriff didn't.

"I'm gonna cut off access to all of them but Mrs. Kraus."

"Hang on," English said. "I don't think you should do that. We're loading Mrs. Kraus on a different computer and we've got access to Mad Dog's account. If you leave us the opportunity, someone might contact us on the game again. Maybe give away something that will let me catch him quicker."

"You're on," the tech told him. "But let me know how this comes out. And if you need to cut someone off, call me back."

The sheriff agreed, then rushed the conversation to a conclusion when his cell started ringing. It was his missing daughter. He went straight past the usual pleasantries. "Are you all right?"

"I can take care of myself," she said. The sheriff translated that to mean she'd been involved in stuff he'd rather not know about but had emerged relatively unscathed. She proceeded to confirm just that. Even going way beyond what his vivid imagination had considered. Her car trip with a professional assassin was especially what a worried father wanted to hear, even if Hailey had been along for the ride. But what the killer told her, that might be useful.

"Promise me you'll call the Tucson Police Department right now," he told her.

"What's that?" she replied. "You're breaking up on me."

"Now," he commanded. "Call Sergeant Parker. She won't lock you out of the investigation." He gave her the number.

"Walker? You want me to call someone named Walker?"

"Sergeant Parker, TPD. And cut out this lone-wolf stuff, even when you've got a lone wolf for backup."

"I'm only catching a few words, Dad. I think my batteries must be going."

"Yeah, sure. Promise me you'll call Parker," he said.

"I love you, Dad." And that was it. Her line went dead.

He'd call Parker, then, and tell her roughly where Heather was, since roughly was all he knew. And, as soon as that was done, he had to get out of here. There were six kids he needed to interview. But he would go back over to the courthouse first. If Billy and Cole Macklin were involved, their father had to know about it. That was where he'd left the man less than half an hour ago.

He was pressing the buttons on Doc's second line with Parker's cell number when the entrance to the clinic opened on a huge figure that occupied nearly as much space as the door. The person stood, stooped, head ducked and kind of tucked between his shoulders. Just a kid, though, no matter how large. It took the sheriff a moment to recognize him because the kids he didn't come into contact with in the line of duty were nearly always more mature than the way he remembered them.

"Sheriff English," the monstrous child said in a halting voice. "I've got a confession to make."

This had to be the Ball kid, even though the sheriff was sure Frank Ball had been at least a foot shorter the last time they crossed paths.

"Yes?"

"Well…you see…."

"The sheriff's too busy for nonsense," Mrs. Kraus interrupted. "Spit it out, son."

The big kid snuffled a little. And then he said it. "I'm Fig Zit."

◇◇◇

Heather was wondering how to get back to the university area. A cab, maybe, if Tucson's cabs ran at this time of night. She had her cell phone, but not a local directory. While she was wondering where she might find a booth with a phone book, a pair of headlights turned onto her street at the stop light behind her and headed her way. She could try hitchhiking. In the dead hours of the morning, in a city she didn't know—that would really thrill her dad.

She didn't put out a thumb or wave or do anything else to attract the vehicle's attention, but it slowed and pulled over to the side of the street beside her. It didn't look particularly threatening. It was an ancient, rusted-out VW Bus—evidently a survivor of those long ago days before Heather was born, if its fading paisley flowers and peace signs were any indication. A door squeaked open on the traffic side of the street—if there'd been any traffic—and Ms. Jardine came flying around the front of the vehicle. She wore sweats that surprised Heather because they bore Kansas Jayhawk logos. Her braids sparkled in the glow of the headlights. So did a pair of flashy basketball shoes that swallowed her feet and made her pick them up like a skin diver in fins as she stepped onto the curb.

Heather picked up her jaw and asked, "How did you find me?"

Ms. Jardine let go and stepped back and smiled as her Jayhawk's beak and tail bobbled in a way that made it clear that, as usual, the woman wasn't wearing a bra. "She came and got me."

"Uh, she?"

The woman with the improbable hair, unfettered boobs, and oversized shoes clomped back to the Volkswagen. She took hold of the handle and hauled the sliding door open and Hailey bounded out.

"I started worrying about you, out here on your own. So I decided to disguise myself a little and sneak back to the garage and see if my old VW would start up. It did. I've been cruising all over the place ever since. And then I pulled up at that stop light and there she was. Hailey! Well, I never met her, of course, but your mom sent pictures and told me stories. So I knew she'd come to get me, though I figured it was your uncle she'd lead me to."

Heather felt as confused as if she'd just arrived in Oz. Hailey had gone and found Ms. Jardine. That was impossible. Hailey didn't know the woman, couldn't have understood this was the one person in Tucson who would take Heather wherever she wanted to go. And yet the wolf had brought her back and now they had a ride. Talk about your Uncle Mad Dog moments. The man seemed to live a life of serendipitous coincidences—and dangerous encounters.

"Hailey came for you?"

"Well, I was trying to decide which way to turn at that inter-section and then, there she was, sitting in the road, blocking my way. It took me a minute to figure out who she had to be, but when I said her name she ran up to my door. I opened it and she gave me some kisses, jumped in, and started whining and looking in this direction. Now, here we are."

"I, uh…." Heather was in a realm beyond rational response.

"Come on, honey. I think Mad Dog needs you."

Hailey was back in the bus, whining impatiently.

Heather shrugged her shoulders. What could you do? Ms. Jardine climbed behind the wheel and Heather slipped in beside her.

"Well," Heather said, "I'm not sure where we're going, but let's get started."

◇◇◇

"Drop the gun, asshole!" the cop shouted at Mad Dog, who was about as sure of what to do next as Dorothy must have been on arriving in Oz. That cop sounded like he seriously wanted Mad Dog to give him an excuse to shoot. And Mad Dog sure wanted to put the gun down, but not anywhere near the guy who'd just had plans for it. Not even near the woman who was still kicking, punching, and scratching him, defending her would-be murderer. Mad Dog had a whole new appreciation for his brother's lack of enthusiasm for domestic situations.

"I do mean now," the cop shouted, but the girl had gotten one hand around the barrel and was yanking it so that it was pointed back at her, even though Mad Dog's hand was on the cylinder part instead of the butt and he didn't have a finger near the trigger. If he let go, she'd take it. And considering how she'd just tried to bite his nose, he wasn't confident she wouldn't shoot him. If the cop didn't take care of that first.

Mad Dog started to explain that he *was* trying to put the gun down when the cop screamed for him to let go of the girl, too. Mad Dog dearly wanted to separate himself from the girl, but had a bad feeling the moment she wasn't between him and the cop, the officer would try to put him down.

The whole thing was so ridiculous and such a catastrophe that Mad Dog found himself wondering what someone else might do in this situation, and then recalled the question so many evangelicals in his part of the world were inclined to ask.

What would Jesus do? It gave Mad Dog an inappropriate attack of the giggles.

Well, Jesus probably wouldn't laugh at some unhinged, almost-murder victim, or the policeman who wanted to shoot him.

The good thing about it was, between his giggles and her contortions, Mad Dog lost his balance and they fell against the legs of the guy who had planned to explosively fertilize the yard with her brain. The three of them collapsed into a confused heap on the porch steps. On either side of those steps was a thick mass of pyracantha bushes. Pyracantha has at least as many thorns as whatever they made Jesus' crown out of, but Mad Dog didn't worry about that as he went scrambling behind one of the bushes, aiming for the edge of the house. Neither member of the domestic violence team chose to follow him. He left the pistol in a crotch of branches among a bouquet of thorns and exited at the end of the porch, bleeding from a thousand punctures he hadn't even felt. The problem was, a pair of large black shoes waited just beyond, spread in a shooter's stance. They were topped by neatly pleated uniform pants and a familiar voice that said, "Assault with a deadly weapon, resisting arrest. Talk about a clean shoot." He heard the double click of a hammer being drawn back and wished this wasn't happening because he didn't want to go out in a way that would embarrass his brother.

And, of course, that caused Mad Dog to start giggling again. After all, what Jesus would have done to get out of this would have to be some kind of miracle, right? A miracle was exactly what Mad Dog needed right now.

◇◇◇

The sheriff grabbed the edge of the desk and pulled himself to his feet. Mrs. Kraus had gone quiet. Obviously, she'd overheard the boy's claim to be Fig Zit.

"Come on in, Frank," the sheriff said. "Let's you and me borrow one of Doc's back rooms. Sit down and talk about this."

Frank slouched into Doc's office. He had to be at least six-four and 250 pounds, but he moved like a small child toward an appointment out behind the tool shed. He managed to look up shyly at the sheriff by tucking his head so deeply into his chest he would otherwise be staring at his shoes.

The sheriff manhandled his walker down the hall. He tested the first door he came to and it opened on a standard examination room. An elevated table with disposable paper covering gray vinyl upholstery occupied its center. The table was surrounded by a few industrial chairs. A blood pressure cuff hung on one wall. The others were taken up by cabinets and a space where the requisite eye chart hung.

"Have a seat," the sheriff said. Frank moved his bulk through the door and made the room feel suddenly cramped. The boy sat on the paper as reluctantly as if he already knew about prostate exams.

"So you're Fig Zit?" It made sense that one of the people on that list had to be Fig Zit, but this kid, no matter how big he was, bore no resemblance to the character that ran around WOW, frying Madwulf and others.

"Yes, sir." The boy's voice broke and he cleared his throat and said it again with no more self-assurance but without a shift of octaves. "I guess I gotta take the responsibility for inventing him."

The sheriff would have preferred to conduct this interview back at the jail. All those cold iron bars had a way of evening the odds when he knew too little about what was going on. They seemed to prompt the guilty into filling the blank spaces—when the sheriff didn't know what to ask—with justifications that often turned into confessions. This room, while not warm and welcoming, was too neutral for that. Frank might be out of his element, but so was the sheriff. If there were blank spaces in need of filling, Frank could just start reading the eye chart.

"Tell me about the killer," the sheriff said. Best to get straight to that bottom line because he still didn't know what might have happened to his daughter or his brother in Tucson.

"Well," Frank said, "I started off as a phantom sorcerer a couple of years ago. But I got frustrated with how slow you move up in levels and how much time it takes to get the good armor and stuff. So me and some guys, we worked out a way to hack into one of Worldcraft's servers and...."

"Whoa. I don't give a damn about the game. I mean the professional killer you turned loose on Heather and Mad Dog in Tucson tonight."

Frank's eyes got big and he shook his head. "You know about that, too?"

"Sure," the sheriff said. "I've talked to Mad Dog and Heather both. Mad Dog got blamed for one murder and the same killer tried to hurt Heather."

"Nu-uhh," Frank said.

What did that mean? Had he changed his mind about admitting things?

"A cop was killed in Arizona tonight, and in a way that made it look like Mad Dog did it. Then, the same killer made an attempt on my daughter. Talk, Frank. I need to know who this guy is and how to find him."

Frank just sat there, eyes wide, shaking his head.

"I have to know now," the sheriff continued, "because your assassin might still be after either or both of them."

"No way," Frank said. "I mean…are you telling me that was like real?"

It was the sheriff's turn for wide eyes. "You told me as Fig Zit, in that stupid game, you were going to hurt Heather just a few hours ago."

"Not me," Frank said. "Not tonight. I haven't been on War of Worldcraft tonight. But Tucson, I knew about Tucson. That's supposed to be just another game. You mean that's real?"

"A man assaulted Heather a little while ago. Told her he was going to mutilate her, but she got away. It happened just like you told me and Mrs. Kraus it would in that internet game."

"Oh, jeez," Frank said. He jumped to his feet and nearly rammed his head against the ceiling. The sheriff tried to block the door and Frank brushed him aside as casually as the kid's virtual monster destroyed everything it came across.

"Stop!" the sheriff shouted from the floor where he lay tangled up with his walker.

"Stop it. Yeah, got to stop it," Frank said, disappearing down the hall.

There was a time when bringing down someone, even a guy as bulky as Frank Ball, wouldn't have been a problem for the sheriff. Of course that was before a bullet fragment chipped a piece off his spine and caused havoc with the nerves that told his legs what to do. Right now, they told his legs to kick that damned walker across the room and go pounding after the runaway teen who might know how to save Heather's and Mad Dog's lives. His injured nerves were getting better, thanks to what seemed like an endless course of physical therapy. A sudden burst of adrenaline didn't do any harm either. He shoved the walker aside, got to his feet, went through the door. Frank Ball lumbered past Mrs. Kraus while she frantically dug through her purse for her Glock.

He could do it. One quick sprint and he'd tackle the kid at the front door. He got as far as the front room before nerves, adrenaline, and will ran out. The sheriff plowed a furrow in the carpet with his nose.

Mrs. Kraus had found her Glock. "You want me to step outside and shoot him?"

An engine roared to life. Tires bit asphalt. It was too late. Fig Zit had gotten the best of them once again.

◇◇◇

The professional didn't believe in torture, except as a hobby. He'd often thought he might have provided the Bush administration with invaluable insights on the subject. Saved them lots of trouble and embarrassment. Except he didn't work well with others. Not even other assassins.

The problem with torture as a means of acquiring information was that everyone could be broken. And once you broke them, they'd tell you anything you wanted to hear to make it stop. No, if you wanted honest answers, they had to be gained by a frank dialogue, a candid exchange of information that made it clear how those on both sides of the conversation stood to benefit. That's why, when he duct-taped the government employee he'd spoken with earlier to the bed, he didn't bother covering the man's eyes. In fact, after drawing the shades, he'd turned on all the lights so the man could watch him sort through the selection of knives he'd borrowed from yet another Wal-Mart on his way across Tucson. And why he chose an exceptionally large cleaver to hold to his victim's throat as he ripped off the gag and pulled the sock from the man's mouth.

"Softly, softly catchee monkey." The professional whispered the ancient proverb as he held one finger to his lips and pressed the cleaver just hard enough to provide its own thin crimson hint. "If you cry out, I'll open your throat below your larynx. You'll be able to breathe, but you won't be able to make any noise. And you should understand, that would upset me because then I'll have to read your lips when I want you to tell me something."

The guy got it. He made no sound aside from his ragged gasping for breath.

The professional reached down and picked up something sharp and scoop-like. He held it over the man's right eye. "Did you know, if I use this carefully and don't sever the nerves, you'll still be able to see out of your eyeballs after I remove them from their sockets?"

That was too much for total silence, but the professional didn't punish the guy when he whimpered. Clearly, the man was beginning to understand what he had to gain from their conversation. Or merely keep.

The professional switched the scoop for a slender, serrated blade. "Or, that the average human has between twenty and thirty feet of intestines?" He glanced up at the bedroom ceiling. "Enough to loop over your ceiling fan. I wonder what would happen if we did that and then turned the fan on."

"Why?" It was closer to a sob than a question, but it was a wonderful place to begin exchanging information.

"You recall our meeting earlier today."

Clearly, the man did. His eyes had gleamed with abject terror from the moment he woke to find himself helplessly attached to his own bed.

"I was sent to deliver a message. To advise you to remain silent, in spite of your inclination to cut a deal and tell the authorities everything you know."

The man started to nod but the cleaver persuaded him otherwise.

"Then," the professional continued, "I didn't need to know what the message meant or who sent it." He showed the guy another blade, multi-tipped. The professional couldn't imagine what one might do with those tips. His victim apparently could. "But things have changed. Now, I need to know all of that. If you tell me, clearly and concisely, I'll leave you bound to this bed but otherwise unharmed. Do you believe me?"

"Votes," the man whispered.

Obviously, his victim believed. Or hoped. Certainly, he believed the professional wanted to use those knives. And the professional was curious about the fan. But he had no intention of hurting the man unless he lied. The victim appeared to understand that.

"Votes?"

"I work for the elections department. Run the elections computer."

"Ah! So you fixed an election? For whom?"

"Bond issue." His victim was trying to get it out as fast as possible. "For the growth lobby. More profits for developers."

"I don't care about why. I just want to know who. Who paid you?"

"No money." The man winced because the professional didn't believe that and must have pushed a little harder on the cleaver.

"Really," the man said. "Just favors. Investment advice. You know."

The professional did. His victim might have convinced himself he hadn't been bribed, that he'd just done a favor for people who were doing him favors in return. The professional didn't care how someone squared things with their conscience. A payoff was a payoff.

"Names?"

"Tucson Management Alliance. They're a bunch of...."

"Who specifically? Who hired you? Who are you getting favors and advice from?"

"It's never that clear. Really!" The man was desperate to be believed. Desperate enough to give the professional a complex answer because it was true.

"Even when kings gather, there's only one emperor. I think I already know this one's name."

"Bobby Earl Macklin," the man said. "Yeah. He would have called the shots. But I never met him. Just talked to people that work for him."

"I suppose the precise question is who would hire me to pay you a visit this afternoon?"

"Macklin, I guess. But I'd have to say the guys at that internet tech company were probably in on it."

That took the professional by surprise. "Fick's?"

"Yeah. Fick's Internet Technologies. They're the ones who hacked the election. I just followed their instructions. Copied an early ballot count. Took it home. Loaded it on my machine so they could do their fix."

"You know Fick's? You know who they are? You know where I can find them?"

The professional must have pushed on the cleaver again because his victim's voice was harsh when he moaned, "No. Just on the phone. Just internet connections."

"Will Bobby Earl Macklin know how to find Fick's?"

"Yeah. I'm sure of it."

The professional stuffed the sock back in the man's mouth and duct-taped it in place. "I believe you. And I hope you're right. I don't think anyone will find you before I pay a visit to Macklin. If he can't tell me what I require, I'll be back to experiment with my knives."

The man nodded. He wasn't lying. He believed Bobby Earl Macklin would know about Fick's, but he wasn't sure of it. The professional could tell by the way the man kept glancing at the ceiling. But he'd told all he knew without inventing anything. It was enough. If Macklin couldn't tell the professional how to get to Fick's, he would know who could. This guy might be able to give the professional more names, but none who were equal to Macklin. There would be no point coming back here, except self indulgence.

The professional packed up his knives. They might be useful on Macklin. On his way out the door, the professional flicked a switch. The overhead fan hummed as it began to circle and engage his victim's imagination in a way that could make it impossible to ever sleep beneath one again.

◇◇◇

The cop really was going to shoot him. Mad Dog realized his case of the giggles had taken on a touch of hysteria. He tried to look the officer in the eyes and stop laughing long enough to make a rational plea for his life. He didn't get the chance.

"Yeah! Blow his ass away." The male half of the domestic violence team shouted.

"Fucker needs to be killed for attacking my sweet man," the woman said.

And, just like that, the officer changed his mind. There would be no shooting here—not in front of witnesses. It wasn't the kind of miracle Mad Dog had in mind, but he'd take it.

"On the ground," the cop said. Other than trying to take the man's gun away from him, Mad Dog didn't think he had any options. He grabbed dirt and dry grass and the cop put a knee in his back, a gun in his ear, and a pair of steel handcuffs on Mad Dog's wrists—tight against the back of his neck. Then some kind of plastic band secured his ankles. It was all done, slick as a calf roper at a rodeo. Mad Dog half expected the guy to jump to his feet, throw his arms in the air, and wait to hear his time announced. It didn't happen, of course. Instead, the cop patted him down hard enough to make the giggles go away. There was nothing to find, except a billfold, a little change, and a miniature Swiss Army knife.

"Where's the gun, asshole?"

"Their gun?"

"The gun you were holding on this lady. Where'd you stash it?"

"It really is their gun. He was threatening to shoot her and I took it away…."

The cop didn't care. "Where?" He punctuated his question with a short kick to a kidney and Mad Dog decided to tell him.

That didn't win Mad Dog any sympathy, either. The cop shone his flashlight into the veil of thorns and couldn't see it. He didn't seem much inclined to stick a hand in there and feel around. Instead, he ordered Mad Dog to get up. Cuffed and bound, that was easier said than done. Eventually, Mad Dog tottered to an upright position. His feet were too close together for much stability, but he stood there.

The cop backed away into the street and pulled open the back door on his cruiser. "In here."

Mad Dog considered asking how, and then thought better of it. He was alive by the slimmest of threads. This wasn't the moment to argue. So he hopped. The cop grabbed him by an arm and made sure he went through the door head first, half on the floor, half on the back seat. Before Mad Dog could even begin to right himself, the officer used another of those plastic cuffs to pin Mad Dog's ankles to some kind of eye bolt in the floor. The cop slammed the door behind Mad Dog, circled his cruiser, opened the other back door, and did the same for Mad Dog's wrists. That left Mad Dog kneeling awkwardly on the floor as the second door slammed, just after the officer advised him not to bleed on the seats.

That was followed by a confusing time in which Mad Dog discovered he could closely examine a door without a handle or window control or, if he stretched a little, could peer out the side glass at a dark lawn and a big house across the street. A few night lights glowed softly inside and Mad Dog thought about how much he'd rather be there than here. Or, he could listen to the baffling chatter of the blue and white's radio—codes and addresses that meant nothing to Mad Dog. Farther away and muffled, he made out the voices of the young lovers whose affair had been on the verge of coming to a messy end. He picked up just enough to realize they were reinventing the morning's events, winging it and doing a clumsy job of making their stories match. Not that the cop cared. He was just getting the minimum he needed so he could get back to Mad Dog and….

Mad Dog didn't know the answer to that one, but he doubted this couple would wonder, even if they never heard what happened to the guy who'd "assaulted" them on their front porch this morning. Unless they had a reason.

"So sue me," Mad Dog shouted. "No way you'll get more'n a million out of me."

That brought the cop back, and in a worse mood than when he'd left.

"Shut up," he said. And then Mad Dog felt like he'd somehow been beaten on every inch of his body. He had just a moment to wonder if he'd been tasered. Then he was tasered again. Repeatedly.

◇◇◇

"Don't worry," Ms. Jardine told Heather. "We're going to find Mad Dog and he'll be okay."

"You think so?"

"I do. From the things your mother told me about Mad Dog and Hailey, I can't imagine him being in serious trouble if she's here with us. Besides, Mad Dog has a way with people. And he's cute. I had quite a crush on him at one time."

"Really?" Heather was trying to pay attention and be polite, but she had a bad feeling about Mad Dog right now.

"Do you remember the Bull Creek Skinny Dipper?" Ms. Jardine said. "That was me."

That got Heather's attention. The Bull Creek Skinny Dipper had been quite the local scandal for a little while one summer. When Heather was between fourth and fifth grade, she thought.

"You?"

Ms. Jardine laughed as she worked her basketball shoes over the pedals and put the VW through its gears. "I was kind of wild then, or wanted to be. Still had my figure and liked to flaunt it. I was trying to catch your uncle's attention, but it was always somebody else who'd drive by and get an eye full."

"Nobody dreamed it was you," Heather said. Most people thought it was one of the high school girls on a dare. But no one was ever sure. "Nobody could positively identify you."

"Yeah. Well, those who saw me weren't really looking at my face."

"Did you and Uncle Mad Dog…?"

The woman really laughed this time. "Oh, no Heather. He was so wrapped in learning Cheyenne Shamanism then. I think I could have stood on his door step in the altogether and he still wouldn't have noticed me. In fact, I tried that one time. Went to Bertha's Café and picked up some of their fresh sweet rolls. Then I drove out to Mad Dog's wearing nothing but a rain coat and carrying a basket of goodies. I was going to knock on his door and ask him if he'd like some buns, then drop the coat and give him a choice, mine or Bertha's. Only I lost my nerve. Never tried again because he got involved with that widow."

This was fascinating stuff, but it wasn't solving Heather's problems. She knew she should get word to TPD about the psycho. Or to Parker, the way her dad wanted. Then Parker could share what Heather knew with local law enforcement.

"I need to call someone," Heather explained, flipping out her cell phone and punching the number her father had given her. Nothing happened. She checked to see how many bars she had, and whether her battery might be getting low. The battery was at about half staff, which meant she wouldn't be able to talk long. The bars came and went, as if they were weaving through mountain passes instead of rolling straight down a major thoroughfare in the middle of Tucson. Well, crawling, really, since the bus seemed to have problems topping thirty.

"Can't trust electronic things here," Ms. Jardine said. "Even the best technology can't handle the psychic forces around Tucson."

Heather must have given her an odd look.

"There's magic in these desert mountains. Lots of it spills down into the city. That's why there are so many artists here. And why I chose Tucson to open my crystal business."

Heather wasn't beyond considering supernatural explanations, not with an uncle like Mad Dog, but the phone had been working well enough earlier. She'd exaggerated the problem of hearing her dad. Now, she thought it really might be the battery.

"Where do you want to go?" Ms. Jardine asked.

They were headed west, back toward downtown Tucson. It was the direction the psycho had taken. That had been good enough for Heather until now. But it really was something she needed to decide.

"Actually, I don't know," Heather admitted.

"Well, I don't think that's a problem. You may not know where he is. But Hailey surely does."

As if to confirm that, Hailey stuck her head out the window beside Heather's head and let loose a series of yips.

"See?" Ms. Jardine worked her shiny shoes and down shifted. Gears clashing, they edged around the next corner. Heather recognized the street name—Kino. If you went north from here, Kino would turn into Campbell. The university and Ms. Jardine's neighborhood bordered the street. And the University Medical Center was just beyond. That was the last place she'd seen Mad Dog and a reasonable location from which to start looking. And, maybe Ms. Jardine was right. Maybe Hailey knew where Mad Dog was and would lead them there.

Heather decided to do as her dad had asked and check in with Parker. She might get a lead there. She tried the cell phone again. It showed lots of bars as they stopped for the light at Broadway. But her call failed to go through again, and the battery indicator moved down another notch, just from the effort of trying.

"Told you," Jardine said as the light changed.

"Uh, your headlights just went out."

"No big deal," Jardine said. She banged on the dashboard and they came back on. And then she was stomping on the brake to avoid an innocuous gray car that had pulled out of a side street and into their path.

The headlights on the bus lit just in time to spotlight the driver for the briefest moment. The face he turned their way, as he skillfully avoided a collision, was as innocuous as his car. Heather wouldn't have been able to describe him, would have hardly noticed him, except she'd fought him once tonight, then joined him for a drive around Tucson while they pumped each other for information.

"Damn!" Heather said. "It's the psycho."

"Psycho, I'll say he is," Jardine agreed, belatedly pounding on her horn, which evidently worked as irregularly as the headlights.

Hailey added a low growl.

"Follow that car," Heather said.

Jardine laughed. "Sure, as long as he stays in first gear." The woman jammed her foot onto the accelerator and the bus coughed, lurched, died. It took a while to get it restarted, then it refused to exceed thirty-two on the speedometer. The psycho was long gone by the time they got to the south edge of the U of A. By Speedway, his tail lights had become long-term memories.

◇◇◇

Sheriff English pulled his black and white to a stop in front of the courthouse. The building was still dark. The crowd had gone home. There was, of course, no sign of Supervisor Macklin's car. The man must have come only out of curiosity, the sheriff realized. Without power to the building, he couldn't work and there was nothing to keep him there. English pulled out his cell phone, found the supervisor's number in his address book, and punched the call button furiously.

"Macklin," a voice answered.

"Mr. Supervisor. This is Sheriff English. I owe you an apology."

"Yes, you do."

"I'd like to come deliver it to you, sir. Are you home?"

"You really have gone bananas, haven't you sheriff? This is not an appropriate time."

"Listen," the sheriff said. "I need to talk to you and your boys right away. Where are you?"

"Have you been drinking, man? Never mind. I don't care. I'll be calling an emergency meeting of the board at ten this morning to consider your behavior and your role in tonight's catastrophe. Be there. In the meantime, leave me and my sons alone."

"Sir, I don't have that option," the sheriff began, but he was talking to dead air.

What to do? The supervisor lived two miles south of town. It could take ten minutes to cross Buffalo Springs and get there, then more time to get back if the Macklins weren't home. After that, still more time would be required to find another of the kids who might be involved. All of them lived in or near town, but he could waste a lot of precious minutes before he found the right one. Or they might all be involved. But his money was on the Macklins. Especially after Heather told him about the connection with that businessman in Tucson. Maybe Mrs. Kraus could get the man to….His cell rang and he popped it open and found Mrs. Kraus was one step ahead of him.

"I got him," she said. "He's right here."

"Got who?"

"Fig Zit," she said. "He's standing here, right in front of me."

"The Ball kid came back?"

"No," she was breathing fast. "The monster in the computer. I've got him on my screen right now. He's telling me what he's gonna do to me. Got me, my character that is, paralyzed and unable to fight back. Keeping me just barely alive while he tells me how he's gonna come over here to Doc's office and rip my heart out."

"He knows it's you, Mrs. Kraus?"

"Oh, yeah. Says even my Glock won't be no help against his magic because it doesn't just live in the computer. Says he'll be coming through the door any minute…."

"Does he know I'm not there?"

"Yes. He's taking special pleasure in telling me how, when he's done with me, he's going after you."

"Mrs. Kraus, those boys don't live where they could have seen me leave Doc's office. Or seen me between there and the courthouse. So how…?"

"Hold on. I'm getting one of them whispers down in the corner. It's that tech at Worldcraft. Hot damn! He's redefining my character. Replacing my armor with stuff that's well nigh impervious. Giving me some weapons they haven't even released into the game yet. And, he says the only user in our area who's logged on right now is the Miller boy."

That couldn't be. The Millers lived out of town. Isaac Miller couldn't know where the sheriff was. Or couldn't know from home. But he might know if he were at the We Fix It shop on Main. The sheriff hadn't thought of that. Ed Miller, the man who'd bombed his brother's place and the courthouse, had lived in a converted shed out back of the shop. Isaac Miller and his family lived out near Mad Dog. But evidently Isaac was at the shop.

"Keep him busy, Mrs. Kraus," the sheriff said, spinning a U-turn in front of the courthouse and pointing his cruiser toward Main Street.

"You bet I will," Mrs. Kraus said. "I just shrunk him down to pint-sized and stuffed a rancid weretoad up his nose. He ain't doing much threatening at the moment."

The sheriff should have activated his lights and siren on the two blocks back to Main Street. But he was already yanking his door open and maneuvering himself, his walker, and a sawed-off shotgun out the door before he thought about it. There were lights on behind the blinds drawn over the windows in the front of We Fix It. And excited voices exchanging blame just inside. The sheriff reached down and tried the door knob. It wasn't locked.

◇◇◇

Mad Dog was faintly aware of movement. He was in a car, but he couldn't remember why or where it was going.

And then the car stopped and someone opened a door behind him and did something to his feet. They closed that door and came around the car and opened another door. Someone applied snips to a plastic cord attached to his hand cuffs. Where had the hand cuffs come from? In fact, where was he and how had he gotten here?

"Get out of the car."

That would be the cop who'd decided not to kill Mad Dog. It was beginning to come back to him now, or bits of it. One of the things he remembered was the cop had never told him he was under arrest or read him his rights. He thought about complaining about that and then remembered the taser.

"Get out of the car, I said."

Mad Dog tried and couldn't get his muscles to cooperate. He only managed to topple over on his face. It hurt, but he already hurt so many places that this new one didn't matter much.

The cop grabbed Mad Dog by his collar at the nape of his neck and dragged him out the door. Mad Dog managed to get his cuffed hands under him and keep his face from dragging along the sidewalk. But even when the cop tried to lift him, Mad Dog couldn't get his feet under himself in order to stand. Finally, the cop gave up and left Mad Dog kneeling. He watched a drop of blood fall from his nose and splash on a cracked sidewalk through which a few bits of dry Bermuda grass poked and waited patiently for rain.

The cop stepped away from Mad Dog for a minute and then there were two cops. Each one grabbed Mad Dog by a shoulder. They dragged him up an ancient flight of concrete stairs to what seemed to be a loading dock, then over to a battered wooden door that a guy in a suit held for them. There was a hall, and at the end of it, another door. Inside that, an office. At least that was what it said on the pebbled glass that made up its top half. No one had labeled offices this way for the last half century and that made Mad Dog think he probably wasn't someplace they were going to offer him a phone call or an attorney.

Mad Dog didn't get much of a look at the place before the two men shoved him. He lost his balance and ended up on his hands and knees, facing a scuffed wooden floor. His muscles wouldn't cooperate yet, but his mind had begun grasping details again, and trying to sort them out.

"He was as good as dead, Chief, then he started shouting lawsuit. Got some citizens interested. So I brought him in, like you said."

Chief? Mad Dog didn't get it. If the police chief was here, Mad Dog should be in jail, getting fingerprinted and photographed and having his belt and shoelaces confiscated.

"No problem," someone said. "I know what we'll do with him."

Mad Dog managed to raise his head. He could sense the two cops who'd carried him in, one at either shoulder. They were both in uniform—shoes, pleated slacks. A big man in a cheap suit leaned against the edge of the desk. Another, in the kind of suit you couldn't get off the rack, sat behind it. The standing one opened his mouth and spoke—a smoker's voice.

"So, Dempsey, you got someone else in mind for him to kill before we nail him in the act?"

Dempsey? Was he the guy behind the desk? Was he a police chief? None of this made any sense.

"Yeah. He'll kill another cop," the man who might be chief said. "I'm thinking he'll make another attempt on Parker. And succeed this time, though we'll take him down in the process."

◇◇◇

Parker's cell rang, interrupting her discussion with Captain Matus. She'd swung by University Hospital to see what was happening in the hunt for Mad Dog and found the captain in need of a ride. And, more importantly, the captain had become an ally, someone else who wanted to find Mad Dog for a reason other than to gun him down.

They sat in her car near the Campbell Avenue exit, comparing notes and planning strategy. So far, they'd come up pretty much blank on the strategy thing. Campbell was dead empty. No one had gone by recently, not since a little silver car flew past heading north.

Parker's cell rang and she snapped it open and answered. All she got was lots of static.

"Hello," Parker said. "Anyone there?"

The static crackled back at her in a way that almost sounded like words.

"You're breaking up. Say again."

She held the phone away from her and checked the caller's number. It was showing a Kansas area code.

"...arker? Is...you?" her cell phone crackled.

It sounded like a woman's voice.

"Hello, Sergeant Parker here," she said, but the signal was gone again, lost to static and finally silence.

"I think that was Heather English," she told Matus.

"Good," he said. "She's got my car keys."

Parker's cell rang again. "Heather?" she answered.

"Who? Is that you, Parker?" Assistant Chief Dempsey's voice held all the warmth of deep space.

"Yes, sir."

"I understand you're in the field looking for this Mad Dog guy."

Parker turned and looked at Matus. "If you're speaking of Mr. Harvey Edward Mad Dog, Chief Dempsey, yes. Captain Matus of the Sewa Tribal Police and I have joined up to try to locate him."

"Matus is with you? Well, that's fine. Real fine. Anyone else?"

"No," Parker said.

"Good. I think I can put you on this Mad Dog's trail," the Chief said. "He's been spotted in the downtown area. If you get right down here, you and Matus may be able to help us talk him in."

Dempsey was the guy who'd issued the force's coded shoot-to-kill order. Had he changed his mind? Had he decided she and Matus were right and Mad Dog might not be a killer after all? The man was a misogynist and a fool, but he hadn't risen through the bureaucracy by making catastrophic mistakes like this one with Mad Dog.

"We can be there in five minutes, sir."

"Good," Dempsey said. He gave her an address and told her he'd meet them out front. "Hurry. I need you here before the SWAT team assembles. You understand?"

She did. "On our way," she said.

"Mad Dog?" Matus' eyebrows raised with the question.

Parker nodded, folding her cell back into its holster.

"Then let's go."

Parker hit the accelerator. There was only one vehicle moving anywhere within sight and it was on the far side of the street. She didn't bother turning on her flashing lights or her siren, and never gave the old flowered VW bus a second glance.

◇◇◇

The sheriff went into the Fix It shop behind his shotgun. It wasn't necessary. There were no armed people inside. Not unless you counted the one on the monitor. Mrs. Kraus' avatar, towered over a teddy bear-shaped imp with Fig Zit's face. The mini-Fig Zit ran around in circles while hearts and flowers bloomed in the air about its head.

Inside the room, two teenage boys remained completely oblivious to the sheriff and his shotgun, shouting back and forth at each other across a pair of keyboards and enough ultra-modern computer equipment to launch a global nuclear war.

"How could…?"

"Why won't…?"

"Got to…"

"Security wall…"

The sheriff made his way into the room. "Step away from the computers," the sheriff said. "Lie flat on the floor and put your hands behind your heads."

"Analyze code…," one said.

"New hack…," the other interrupted.

The sheriff thought about putting a round through their monitor to see if that might get their attention, but the screen went suddenly blank all by itself. A flashing LOST SIGNAL message appeared and shut off the flood of their voices.

"You're under arrest. On the floor. Now!" the sheriff shouted.

"Cable's down," one said.

"Can't be." The other kid actually jumped to his feet and ran past the sheriff to the door without appearing to notice anyone was there. "Somebody cut it." He shoved some blinds aside and peered out onto Main Street. A familiar engine started out there. The boy confirmed it. "Frank. Frank Ball cut it at the pole."

The sheriff leaned over and slapped one cuff on that kid's left wrist. He attached the other to the handle of a roto-tiller that, according to the tag, Pete King had brought in for repair.

"This can't be happening," the remaining boy chanted, over and over, like a mantra. The sheriff used his spare set of cuffs to fasten the kid to the swivel chair he occupied.

That finally got the boy's attention.

"You didn't have to do that, sheriff," he said. "It's only a game."

◇◇◇

Bobby Earl Macklin was proud of his little ten-thousand-square-foot ranch-style house in the Catalina foothills. North of Skyline, of course, with the back of the property butting up against the Coronado National Forest and far enough from the new La Encantada shopping center for privacy. It sat on twenty acres of prime foothills real estate, fenced, posted with warnings, and equipped with better security than the new fence along the nearby Mexican border. He had a little private army for just in case, and a number of sound-proofed rooms—office, bedroom, his wife's bedroom, and, of course, the hobby room.

When he admitted it, Bobby Earl was on the back side of sixty, While he had lost most of his interest in Mrs. Bobby Earl, despite all the nipping and tucking those ridiculously expensive cosmetic surgeons had done, he still lusted in his heart after the young ladies. The very young ladies, actually. Considering his lofty position in Tucson's society, and state and national politics, that lusting was best kept out of the public eye. He'd made some special arrangements with his security folks. Didn't hurt that his wife wasn't even aware of the underground hobby room, either, or its very private entrances and exits.

Bobby Earl had spent the night in that hobby room. Took him longer, these days, to indulge his hobby. Even when a spectacular Lolita dropped by after he rose from a healthy post-dinner nap. With some designer erectile "function" drugs, as he preferred to call them, and a high-dollar contract with the young lady's manager guaranteed to make her eager to please, it had still taken four and a half hours of sweaty effort before he satisfied his needs. Only then did he notice how exhausted and unsatisfied his young companion actually was. He would have thought she could manage a bit of pretense for what he was paying, and maintain it long enough to be escorted out. He was mentally lowering the tip he'd planned to reward her with as he buzzed for his social secretary. Time to get the real girl out of here so he could concentrate on the memories—her perfect little body, her truly amazing flexibility—and forget her clear disappointment in his performance.

"Bobby Earl Macklin, I presume?"

The voice was not his social secretary's. Nor any of his security team members.

"And your granddaughter?"

The wise-ass comment made it clear the man didn't work for him, or wouldn't after tonight.

The girl giggled, shimmied back into her pleated jumper, and pulled on her Mary Janes. Bobby Earl decided she wasn't getting any gratuity whatsoever. He sat up in the satin sheets of his mirror-surrounded bed and found the reflection of half a dozen small, trim, and generally uninteresting men standing over in the room's main entrance. Of course, no one who'd entered this room uninvited or unescorted could be truly uninteresting.

Bobby Earl sucked in his gut, rearranged the sheets, and scooted to the edge of the bed as he turned to face the man. Bobby Earl kept a Taurus .454 five-shot pistol in a secret compartment on this side of the bed, just in case a Cape Buffalo happened to get in here, or some human he didn't care for. This guy was so small the Taurus would probably cut him in half.

"You her pimp?" Bobby Earl saw no reason to be polite. Under other circumstances, he would have used the term manager. But he didn't deal with managers. His social secretary took care of those details. Where the hell was that man, anyway?

Bobby Earl couldn't imagine how any stranger other than the girl's manager could be on his property. The girl had come with an escort of course—her manager, or what Bobby Earl had just called him. Bobby Earl supposed his security people must have relaxed a little and let the bastard slip in. Heads would roll. He pushed a button under the edge of the mattress that would bring them running, then felt for the hidden spot where the .454 resided.

"No. I'm not her pimp. I'm your fix it man."

That didn't clear anything up for Bobby Earl. The girl, dressed now, sat on the edge of the bed and sucked a thumb while she waited for whatever might happen next.

"Fick's Internet Technologies," the man explained. "You and they arranged for me to fix it. And I did. I paid a visit on your elections man. And I took care of that item at Pascua Yaqui Village."

If this man was who he claimed, well, Bobby Earl wanted that Taurus in his hand in the worst way. He grabbed for it and suddenly found himself bent over backward across a stack of pillows beside an assortment of velvet whips. The girl had looked much better in the reflections his mirrors showed when she was in a similar position an hour or so earlier. And when Bobby Earl appreciated those reflections, there had been no small trickle of blood at the corner of her mouth.

"You 'bout to regret that," Bobby Earl said. The small man's reflection didn't seem concerned. In fact, he wasn't paying attention. He was speaking to the girl.

"Hi," he asked her. "What's your name?"

Bobby Earl would take special pleasure in what his security force did to this guy. He had a couple of former special ops people, one with experience in interrogations in Afghanistan. He'd let them get creative with the intruder. They'd know how to make the guy suffer…. Only, where the hell were they? Two armed men should have come busting in here less than sixty seconds after he punched that button. Surely it had been longer than that already.

"My name's Taylor," the girl said.

Taylor? Where the hell did she come up with a name like that? Bobby Earl wondered if maybe he should have asked her name himself. Not that it mattered now.

"Taylor," the stranger told her, "you're a very pretty girl. And you're likely to stay that way and live a long and healthy life."

Bobby Earl sat up. The trim man never even turned to look at him.

"That's especially true if you don't know what happens in this room in the next few minutes."

"I could leave," the girl offered.

"I'd like to let you go," the man said. "But there's a man sitting in a chair in front of a ruined security console upstairs and I've got it fixed so, if he moves, he'll ground a live wire and electrocute himself. I'd rather you didn't go through that room and disturb him."

"What about…?"

"Your friend? The one who brought you here? I'm afraid he and the rest of Mr. Macklin's security people are in similarly awkward situations. I'd let you leave, but I'm sure you understand I can't have you wandering around in the desert when I don't have time to keep an eye on you."

The girl stared at him with a puzzled, dull look. The kind that wasn't unexpected on a pre-teen you kept up until just before dawn. "You want me to hide under the bed or shut my eyes or something?"

"Shutting your eyes would be good. And duck your head under the covers. Put your fingers in your ears. Maybe hum your favorite song so you can honestly tell people you don't know what's about to happen between Mr. Macklin and me. Do that until I come get you or you count to ten thousand, whichever comes first. All right?"

"Okay," she said. She crawled under the down comforter at the foot of the bed and began humming something Bobby Earl thought was probably rap. He hated rap.

"So, what is this?" Bobby Earl asked. "Billy and his Kansas kiddy corps turn on me, decide they want a bigger piece of the pie?"

The plain man turned toward Bobby Earl, reached under his jacket, and pulled out a serrated knife that gleamed in the room's soft, indirect light. He leaned over and looked straight into Billy Earl's eyes

"I want to know every single thing you can tell me about Fick's I.T. And, if it relates, Billy and that Kansas kiddy corps. Show me that courtesy, Mr. Macklin, and I'll keep quiet about the election you rigged. You'll have the option to do the same, or not, your choice, because I won't have cut your tongue out."

Bobby Earl Macklin had been buying and selling for decades. Property, food, cars, homes, people. He knew a bottom-line offer when he heard one. He spilled his guts, including every detail about Billy and Fick's this stone-cold killer could possibly want to know.

◇◇◇

"So this is the guy who led us on such a merry chase," Dempsey said, coming around the desk and standing over the bald Kansan. "Doesn't look so tough now, kneeling there, drooling on the floor."

One of his uniforms laughed, but up close, Dempsey had to admit the guy was big and muscular enough to be trouble. But not right now. That wasn't really drool, though, it was blood leaking from the man's nose. And the guy was making progress at trying to stand. Getting his legs under him, little by little.

"How many times you stun him?"

"Lost count," the officer admitted.

"More'n they recommend," the other uniform suggested.

No question about that, Dempsey thought. You had to hit a guy a lot of times to leave him this fucked up twenty or thirty minutes later. And with all that, the guy might be about to make it to his feet. Dempsey put a shoe on the man's shoulder, pushed, and toppled him easily.

"Let's get this over with." Dempsey's plain-clothes detective didn't like what they were doing. He'd gotten involved because his kid was turned into a paraplegic in a traffic accident that had been his own fault. Even the city's generous insurance had proved insufficient long ago. The detective might be ashamed of himself, but he'd do whatever it took to care for his son.

"This thing's already too fucked up," the detective said. "What were the chances that hit man would take down one of our enforcers at Pascua? Or that we'd spend the whole night chasing this hick around town? Let's just get him out on the tracks and put one between his eyes."

Dempsey thought the Sewa officer who died at Pascua had been about to rat them out. That he'd been thinking about turning state's evidence, along with the elections guy. Not that Dempsey knew for sure. So he avoided that part of the question. "No, we're going to wait and include Parker and Matus. And we won't do it too close to here. I don't want word about our private 'substation' getting out."

"Fourth Avenue?" the detective suggested. "Where the hippies hang out?"

The problem with the hippies was some of them might still be hanging out, or starting their day early.

"No. The three of you, take him to the parking garage at Pennington and Scott. Third level, central staircase. I'll get my car and wait for Parker and Matus. I'll send them up. Be ready. Take them from behind with one gun. Turn another on this guy. Make it look good."

The detective nodded, all business. The uniformed officers high-fived each other, like they were about to take the field for the annual interdepartmental softball tournament.

"Need a throw down?" Dempsey asked.

"Got a spare .45," the detective said. "Good one, so we'll be sure of Parker and Matus."

"Then go. Set it up. I'll be right behind you with this cop-killer's last victims."

The uniforms took the bald guy by the shoulders and jerked him to his feet. He tried to walk, but he wasn't ready for it yet.

"You'll clean up here?" the detective asked from the door.

Dempsey hadn't planned on it, but the man was right. There were a few other officers who knew about this place, but not this situation. Before long, all of them would have heard about Parker and Matus and Mad Dog. There shouldn't be any fresh blood stains on the floor in here.

"Yeah. I got it."

The detective disappeared down the hall in the wake of the uniforms and their prisoner. Dempsey went to the utility closet. He grabbed a mop, ran some water in a bucket, and mixed in cleaning solution. He did a half-assed job, but it wasn't like no one had ever bled on this floor before.

He put the cleaning stuff away and was about to leave the building when his cell rang. Were Parker and Matus already here? He snatched the phone off his belt and checked to see who was calling, then answered real quick. You didn't keep Bobby Earl Macklin waiting.

"Mr. Macklin. What can I do for you?"

"Where are you? What's going on?" Tucson's biggest wheeler dealer's voice sounded harsher than usual.

"The office in the warehouse by the tracks. We've got that Mad Dog. We're setting up another incident to establish him as a psycho."

"Right." Macklin paused. "Where's it going down?"

Dempsey told him.

"Wait for me."

It wasn't like Macklin. Usually, he didn't want to know any details when they had to get their hands dirty, let alone turn himself into a witness.

"Hey, you sure you want this?"

"Wait!"

"Okay, sir. But this could get messy. We got targets coming for him. Gonna be hard to keep them occupied for long."

"Won't be long. But, by damn, Dempsey, you better wait for me."

"Sure, sure, no problem," Dempsey said, but by then, no one was on the other end to hear him.

◇◇◇

"Only a game?" English said. He was tempted to slap the kid upside the head a few times—with a two-by-four, maybe.

"Yeah. Another one, like War of Worldcraft, only better," the Peirce kid said from where he sat in front of a monitor. Isaac Miller was by the door, attached to the roto-tiller.

"Killing a cop is a game?"

"Kill a cop, kill a dragon," the Miller boy said, "what's the difference? They just respawn if we want them back. Then they're right back in the game."

The sheriff shook his head. Did these kids really believe that? Frank Ball had seemed to start with a similar opinion.

"Listen to me," English said. "A policeman died in Tucson tonight. Mad Dog is on the run down there, accused of the murder. And my daughter…."

"Oh sure. We know. It's because of our assassin."

"Your assassin?"

"In our game, Sheriff. It's a computer game we've been developing. It'll be out there, competing with Syms and Halo and WOW one of these days. But while we're refining it, it's more fun to throw in characters we know from real life. That's why we decided to put Mad Dog and Heather at risk tonight. We probably wouldn't kill them off, even in a game, but it's just their avatars that are at risk." His shrug was obscenely casual. "Just a bunch of ones and zeros in the electronic ether."

"No," the sheriff said. "I'm telling you, a real policeman died a real death. Not make believe. My daughter was actually attacked by some kind of maniac, and my brother truly is being chased by officers who think he's a cop killer. Not in those computers of yours. Not avatars. Not electronic ether. Real people! In Tucson!! Right now!!!"

"No way," Isaac Miller said.

"That can't be," Kevin Peirce echoed.

"Yes. That cop is irreversibly dead. And don't you know about the bomb at the courthouse?"

"Well, sure," Peirce said, though he didn't sound as certain of himself anymore. "It's more fun when we make some of the stuff happen in the real world, but that was just an M-80 and…."

An M-80 was a super firecracker, though big and dangerous enough to be illegal in Kansas.

"It wasn't an M-80," the sheriff said. "It was a Bouncing Betty, Vietnam War ordnance like that M79 grenade that blew my brother's house off the face of the earth earlier this morning. Really destroyed it, just like thousands of others killed real people in real wars."

"You're not serious," Peirce said, though his eyes had begun to take on the fearful look of someone afraid the opposite was true.

"And Ed Miller," the sheriff continued, "is every bit as dead as that cop in Tucson, burned to a crisp when the thing bounced off the courthouse wall and exploded in his face. Doc Jones is opening his chest and skull, or what's left of them—doing an autopsy, even as we speak."

"But Billy said…" Peirce muttered.

"No," Miller said. "That's wrong. It can't be because that'd mean…."

"You're responsible for two deaths," the sheriff said.

Kevin Peirce shook his head. "Way more'n two. We've been running assassins for a year."

"Oh Jesus," Isaac Miller moaned. "Did we fix real elections? Did Uncle Ed truly die?"

The sheriff nodded.

"Wow!" Peirce said. "Does that mean I moved real millions into those offshore accounts?"

◇◇◇

"Turn left," Heather said, indicating the parking lot near the hospital's emergency room entrance. "I've got a faster car here."

"Sure," Ms. Jardine said. "But where are we going that we've got to hurry?"

Heather wished she had a good answer. She'd almost gotten Parker the last time she tried. She dialed again as Ms. Jardine pulled the VW in an empty slot. Nothing. The battery symbol indicated no charge at all.

"Shit," she said, and stuffed the phone back in her fanny pack.

"Look at Hailey," Ms. Jardine said. "She's not worried so you needn't be."

Hailey didn't seem upset. Impatient, maybe, but she sat on the back seat and waited without complaint.

"Funny," Heather said. "I really thought she might lead us to Mad Dog."

"Still could."

Heather got out of the bus and trotted to Matus' 4Runner, three slots down. Hailey was right behind her, but as Heather fumbled with the key, Hailey passed her and kept going.

"Hailey!" Heather called. The wolf didn't look back or slow down.

Ms. Jardine joined her, basketball shoes slapping the asphalt. "Like now, maybe," she said.

"Get in." Heather yanked her door open and jumped behind the wheel.

Ms. Jardine ran around the SUV and did as she was told. "You know what to do now?" she said, climbing into the passenger's seat.

Heather twisted the key and the engine roared. "Damn right I do. Follow that wolf."

◇◇◇

"Mad Dog was on the floor in the back of another police car. Not a marked one, this time. But big. A solid dark-blue sedan with four doors that screamed official-government-vehicle for all its lack of insignia.

He didn't know where they were going. Not far, if he'd understood what was happening back in that warehouse. Not that he was sure he had. His mind was as confused and unresponsive as the rest of his body. He thought they were going to a parking lot. For his execution. And someone else's. Parker's he thought. And…? He tried to concentrate. To remember. To decide how to get out of this.

One of the uniformed officers was in the back with him. The man sat, keeping him pressed to the floor by planting big feet in the middle of Mad Dog's back. Not that he would have been doing push ups back here, anyway. He ached. Every single muscle felt like it had just been through the most vicious workout of his life. Even his eyebrows hurt.

At least he wasn't confined by cuffs anymore. They'd taken those off before they hauled him into the office. But he wasn't sure they hadn't replaced them with plastic before putting him in the car. Streetlights went by, alternating moments of light and dark. He couldn't see anything with his face pressed to the floor between the front and rear seats. He made sure about the cuffs by stretching his hands farther apart than he could have if a binding were there. Then he folded one leg up toward his butt while keeping the other against a back door. The cop kicked it down. Mad Dog's muscles threatened to cramp, but it was their pain that confined him now, not steel or plastic ties.

The car never got up much speed. And it turned a couple of times before its tires began squealing the way tires often did on concrete surfaces. Like parking garages, for instance. Like they might in the place where these bastards planned to kill him for reasons he didn't begin to understand.

The car stopped. Doors opened. Mad Dog tried to lift his head to see where they were, but he couldn't. The only weapon he had left was surprise. He had to take them off guard. Slug somebody, push somebody, run like hell. If he could. He tried to get his legs under him as they pulled him out of the car and didn't quite manage it. It was going to be hard to run if your body wouldn't obey you any better than that.

No real point in trying, though. Not yet. Not until the right moment. So, he didn't try again. He let them drag him across the oil-stained concrete toward a stairwell near the center of the building.

"Yeah," one of the men said. The one in the suit, not one of the uniforms. Mad Dog realized the man had answered a cell phone. The buzzing he'd thought was just inside his head must have been the phone.

"No shit?" the guy said. Then, "Okay. Whatever."

"What?" one of the uniforms asked.

"We got to wait," the suit told them. "The big man himself wants to come watch us do this one."

"Macklin?"

Mad Dog thought the name sounded familiar. But it had nothing to do with Tucson.

"What I said, wasn't it?"

"That'll be a first."

More time, Mad Dog thought. More time to recover. He could use that because he couldn't stop himself from impacting the concrete with his face when the uniforms dropped him, even though he tried. Mad Dog's nose started bleeding again, and there was blood in his mouth where his teeth had bit into his lip.

"How long?" one of the uniforms wondered.

"Long as it takes. Man's paying the bills."

Longer would be better, Mad Dog thought. Much longer. He rolled his head to one side so he could watch them out of slitted eyes. The uniforms went over and leaned against a concrete wall. The detective stood at the top of the stairs. He held a Colt .45 semi-automatic pistol in his right hand. It was aimed in Mad Dog's direction.

Long enough for that .45 to get really heavy, Mad Dog thought as he spit a little blood and maybe a piece of tooth onto the pavement.

◇◇◇

The moon sliced its way down the Kansas sky behind the sheriff as he approached the Macklin place. It was only a mile and a half southeast of Buffalo Springs and lay near the center of a rich quarter section, ready for a heavily irrigated crop of corn that would feed the ethanol plant. There were only two ways to get there other than cross-country. The long way, going around the section, or the short, direct route. The sheriff chose the latter. But he would have preferred making the trip with some deputies, the full use of his legs, and a better understanding of what he was getting into.

Kevin Peirce and Isaac Miller hadn't been much help. The Peirce kid never quite got it—never fully accepted the idea that what they were doing could be dangerous. And Isaac Miller.... The boy was too shaken by learning what had happened to his uncle. He didn't know where his sister Dana was. He'd believed it was real by the time the sheriff left, but the shock knocked him for a loop. Isaac hadn't been able to calm down and explain things to the sheriff. And the two claimed they hadn't even been on the internet tonight until after the explosion at the courthouse.

It was hard enough for English to grasp the possibility that local teenagers had fixed elections, arranged cover-ups, and run a top-of-the-line hit man to keep their activities from becoming known. Harder still, when, it seemed, the bulk of them hadn't realized they were doing it—at least that it was real. If the sheriff had it straight, only Cole and Billy Macklin might have known. And Dana Miller, maybe. Even Cole might not have fully realized the implications of the things they were doing. Cole was the best hacker among them, but he may have been working on the instructions of his family and the investors behind the ethanol plant.

Times had changed. In the sheriff's memory, the occasional criminals who roamed central Kansas had been forced to do their killing up close and personal, not electronically and without ever encountering their victims or the pawns they used to do the job. Sheriffs who pursued those old-time villains hadn't needed to care about things being played out half a country away.

How would Wyatt Earp or one of his contemporaries have dealt with this? The sheriff shook his head. Same way as usual, he supposed. By buffaloing the opposition—slamming the bad guy over the head with a revolver, disarming him, tossing him in jail, and then leaving a judge to sort it out. Sheriff English hadn't slammed any heads yet, but he'd left Peirce and Miller cuffed to a rototiller and a chair so it'd be difficult for either to make a run for it, or get help without doing some serious explaining. The Ball kid was still out here somewhere, maybe trying to repair the things he'd done. And Dana Miller, Cole and Billy Macklin, and their father the county supervisor…? Well, that was what the sheriff was about to find out.

The patrol car rumbled over a little bridge that crossed one of the many streams feeding nearby Bull Creek. He slowed, and pulled into the drive on the far side of the neatly trimmed evergreens that guarded the south side of the yard. The sheriff's headlights swept across a lawn, thick and neat enough for any fairway even if it was still winter brown. A cluster of stately hardwoods that would soon begin budding out was also illuminated. So was the great porch that circled the sparkling-white Edwardian house at the center of the lot. The sheriff hit the brakes when he realized someone was sitting on that porch. He backed up and centered his headlights on that lonely figure.

There were no lights on in the house. The sheriff thought that was peculiar, since Supervisor Macklin had been awake and over at the courthouse a couple of hours ago. Even if he hadn't come back, the man would have left lights on. Instead, there was no sign of life at all…except for the person in the Adirondack chair, watching him from the porch.

The sheriff popped his door and stood, bringing his shotgun and his walker out behind him. The figure on the porch didn't move. It might have been a mannequin but for the light that reflected from its eyes.

Small figure, short-haired, and wearing some kind of running shoes with stripes that reflected light. Cole, he thought.

The sheriff closed his door and walked up to the edge of his front bumper. He paused there, behind the glare of the headlights, took a flashlight out of his pocket and examined the evergreens behind him, the row of rose bushes at the foot of the porch, and the thatch of some bare-for-the-winter lilacs and forsythia. Nothing.

"That you, Cole?"

Both hands came up and waved, ever so slightly from side to side—a motion that served to confuse more than answer. The boy didn't say anything.

"Raise your hands, son, and come on down off that porch."

The boy didn't comply and didn't speak. Just waved his hands in that strange manner once again.

"You can come down and cooperate. Help me get this thing stopped and under control right now. Or I can come up there and give you reasons to help." There it was, the Wyatt Earp threat, even if the sheriff really couldn't imagine beating on the kid, no matter what the circumstances. Well, no serious blows, anyway.

Didn't matter. The kid stayed where he was and waved again.

"Damn!" the sheriff said. He balanced his walker and the shotgun and started across the yard. It was a long walk, clumsy for a man whose legs didn't work right and who had to manipulate a walker while he held onto a shotgun as well. He was beginning to wish he'd left the weapon on the seat of his cruiser. After all, there was no indication he'd need it to arrest a teen who was just sitting on a porch.

That teen was madly waving his hands, though, back and forth, but just from the wrists as if the rest of his arms were attached to the chair. The sheriff paused and squinted and finally saw the strip of duct tape across the boy's mouth. And more duct tape that firmly held Cole's legs to those of the chair. Probably, his arms, at the wrist, to the arms of the chair, as well.

Maybe his daughters were right. Maybe he really did need to get some eyeglasses.

"Don't move, sheriff."

The voice wasn't Cole's. It came from near the house, over by a corner that wasn't lit by the beams of the cruiser's headlights. It was a familiar voice, though. Frank Ball's.

The sheriff slowly swung the barrels of his gun in Ball's direction.

"You threatening me, Frank?"

"No, sir. I'm not."

"You tape Cole Macklin to that chair?"

"No, sir." The boy's voice was surprisingly small to come from such a large body. "I just discovered him a little bit ago, before I cut the power to this place. Cut the cable, too, and ruined their satellite dish, just in case. They're off line for sure, Sheriff. That part's safe."

"Then why are you telling me not to move?"

"That lawn, Sheriff. After he trussed his little brother up in that chair, Billy Macklin mined it with some of those Bouncing Betties."

◇◇◇

It wasn't easy for Heather to follow that wolf, even in Matus' much faster 4Runner. Hailey didn't limit her route to streets. Heather had to. In the central city, houses, fences, walls, trees, and giant cacti limited even a four-wheel-drive. So Heather followed when she could and guessed when she couldn't. But she and Ms. Jardine managed to keep Hailey in sight occasionally. In fact, they always seemed to catch a glimpse of Hailey just when they needed it most. It was as if the wolf purposefully showed herself to keep them from getting lost.

They crossed Speedway, then threaded the maze of red brick and towering palms that defined the University of Arizona. Most of the campus streets were closed to through traffic, a fact Hailey and Heather ignored. At this unholy hour, they encountered no other drivers, students, or even campus police to care.

South of the campus, they zigged west toward Tucson High School.

"You know," Ms. Jardine said, ever the history teacher, "they built the university first. This was the first high school in Arizona Territory, but it didn't open its doors till after the university."

The knowledge was of very little help when Hailey chose to cut south again, across Tucson High's football field. Heather made a left at the next street and hoped. She got it right. Hailey continued her southwesterly course and crossed Third Avenue just ahead of the 4Runner.

"Nice work," Ms. Jardine said.

"I think I've got her figured," Heather replied, dodging right when Hailey, as expected, cut west again on Eighth Street.

"I believe you do, but...." There was admiration in the woman's voice, and something else as well.

"What?" Heather asked, throwing the SUV around a corner onto Fourth Avenue.

Streetcar rails ran down the center of Fourth. They protruded above the roadway and grabbed the Toyota's knobby tires. The vehicle tried to turn a lot more suddenly than it was designed for. The driver's-side wheels went into the air as the SUV did its best to roll over. Heather fought the steering wheel and managed to get all four tires back down on the road.

"Wow!" Ms. Jardine said as they bounced to a halt. "You might want to think about a career in stunt driving."

Hailey cut across a parking lot in front of a night club on their right. Fourth Avenue was closed ahead of them.

"That's what I was about to tell you," Ms. Jardine said. "Urban renewal."

The Fourth Avenue viaduct, where it went under the railroad tracks, was being reconstructed.

Heather followed Hailey into the parking lot. What had once been an exit onto the street paralleling the tracks was blocked by chain-link fence. Hailey ducked under it and kept going. Heather hit the brakes just in time to avoid hitting the fence.

"Damn! Which way do I go?"

"Got me," Ms. Jardine said as Hailey made her way through the mess of dirt and rubble the ongoing construction had created just beyond. The wolf climbed the grade to the tracks and disappeared on the far side of the berm. "There isn't another crossing till four blocks northwest of here, or maybe ten blocks east and south."

"Shit!" Heather said. She jammed the 4Runner in all-wheel-drive and followed Hailey's path. The Toyota was way too big for the opening Hailey had navigated, but Heather thought it was powerful enough to create its own. It wasn't. The chain-link caught the truck's front bumper and slewed it around and one of the tires found a hole to drop into. And that was it. The Toyota wasn't going anywhere else without the help of a tow truck.

"Well, don't just sit there, kid," Ms. Jardine said. "Your uncle may need you."

The woman could be right. Heather threw the door open and hit the ground running.

◇◇◇

"Delay?" Parker said. She knew the lexicon. Delay meant there'd been a screw up. Something was wrong and she wanted to know what it was.

Dempsey stepped closer to her car and waved in the general direction of the Ronstadt Transit Center. "Hey. It's nothing. He's in a building nearby. We've got him, but he hasn't been secured yet. They just want us to wait a...."

"Bullshit!" Parker said. "You're acting chief. You don't wait for anybody. And Matus and I, we're here because we can persuade Mad Dog to give himself up. If he's not secured, you need us in there now."

"Cool down, Sergeant." Dempsey leaned in her window and got in her face. "You're right. I decide who waits and when. Right now, that's you."

"You don't decide for me, Chief Dempsey," Matus said. He pushed his door open, on the verge of getting out. Parker thought he probably would have done so if he'd known where to go.

And suddenly, all that was peripheral for Sergeant Parker. Something big and silver-grey and lightning-fast flashed across the street on four legs, about a block in front of her. She recognized the wolf even though it had been four years and a thousand miles since they last met.

"Hailey," she whispered.

Dempsey was confused, "What?"

Matus turned her way, curious.

"Shut the door," she told the Sewa. "Please step away from my window and watch your feet, Chief."

Matus obeyed. The chief's face just darkened as he started to sputter something. She didn't give him enough time to say anything comprehensible. She yanked the selector into gear and hit the accelerator—hard, but not quite hard enough to lay rubber.

The doorpost bumped the chief out of her window. The growl of her engine made his shout incomprehensible. She'd find out later whether the rear tires had missed his feet.

Something had gone wrong with this effort to take Mad Dog prisoner and Dempsey had been lying about it. She and Matus hadn't been able to do anything because they hadn't known where to go. They'd had no choice but to wait. That changed when Hailey streaked across the street ahead of them. The wannabe Cheyenne Shaman had an uncommon bond with that animal. Dempsey be damned. If she could follow Hailey, the wolf would lead them straight to Mad Dog.

"What...?" Matus echoed Dempsey's query. Parker threw the vehicle around a corner, fast, but again, avoided breaking tires loose. Close—she had a feeling they were close and she didn't want to announce their presence. Dempsey would probably take care of that, but they might gain some minutes.

"There." She took one hand off the wheel for a second and pointed.

"Is that...?"

"Yeah. Mad Dog's wolf."

The street was meant for one-way traffic going the other way. There was no traffic so it didn't matter. Hailey took the first right and Parker used the advantage of the unmarked unit's horsepower to close in behind her. Hailey went left and Parker followed and then Hailey wasn't there anymore. Parker's foot came off the accelerator.

"In there," Matus said, pointing.

In there was an old department store. The owners had gone out of downtown, and then out of business, decades ago. The building, now a vivid chartreuse, had been converted into a multi-story parking garage. Parker stopped, considered the arm of the gate that kept her car out but hadn't even slowed the wolf. She maneuvered into a spot that blocked, as best she could, all the entrance and exit lanes.

"Let's go," she said, but Matus was already out his door, rounding the hood, and ducking under the wooden arm. Parker drew her SIG Sauer and followed.

◇◇◇

Mad Dog heard that buzzing again. It made a nice harmony with what was going on inside his head. The man who seemed to be in charge of his execution squad, the guy in the suit, reached for his cell again, put it to his ear, said, "Yeah?"

Outside, Mad Dog heard a car, moving fast, coming this way from the sound of it.

"Coming here?" the detective said. The man sounded surprised. The uniforms stepped away from the wall they'd been leaning against and listened intently.

"What about Macklin?" The man's voice was agitated. Something was happening. Their plans were changing. Mad Dog wasn't foolish enough to think it would make things better for him. He considered testing his arms and legs. He was going to have to do whatever he could very soon. But the detective was looking right at him as the man folded his phone shut. Mad Dog decided he didn't want to know if his arms and legs wouldn't work. Either they'd function and he'd make a break for it, or....

"Dempsey says Parker and Matus are on their way," the guy in the suit told the uniforms. "Says this guy's got some kind of big dog and it ran by and they're following it. Here, apparently. Says we should do what we have to do. The hell with Macklin."

Hailey? Coming here? And bringing a posse in her wake? He felt a flood of hope. A flash of dread, too. The wolf and the people following her might get killed because of him.

"Leave him where he lies," the detective said. "Bait. They'll come up the stairwell or the ramp. You two, get your guns out. You're guarding this guy. You just caught him and ordered him to the ground. I'm going up the stairs to the next level. I'll cover you from there. Get their backs to me and I'll do the shooting… unless something goes wrong. Then take them down any way you have to."

"Right," one of the uniforms said.

"What about the dog?" the other asked.

The detective was already climbing the stairs. Outside, that hurrying car stopped, went quiet. Doors slammed.

"There still any charge in that taser of yours?"

The uniform who'd brought Mad Dog in shook his head.

"In mine," his partner said.

"Then just stop it for now. Quietly," the detective said. "We'll kill it later."

◇◇◇

"Bull!" Sheriff English said. "Nobody had time to turn this lawn into a mine field."

"There aren't many," Frank Ball said. "We didn't have many left after we set off a bunch of ordnance up in the sand hills. But Billy Macklin knew things were coming apart. He knew you'd be here soon, so he set his little brother up on that porch to draw you into a trap."

"Bull," English said again and took another step.

The kid on the porch waved his hands again, frantically. Frank Ball yelled, "No, really."

A bunch of local teenagers couldn't have gotten their hands on Vietnam era mines. But they had. One mine had been part of the cobbled together bomb that blew the windows out of the sheriff's office…and killed the man who threw it. Another had been on the front seat of that man's pickup—with the sheriff's name almost literally on it.

"Don't you see?" Ball said. "It's like in the game. You locate a treasure, only it's on an island in the middle of a burning lake. You've got to find a magician who knows the spell that raises a bridge and gets you there and back safely. Games—that's how Billy thinks."

"Games? And I suppose Cole's having fun being tied up on a porch behind a minefield?"

"I'm not arguing with you, Sheriff. I'm still trying to get my head around this being real. But I've done everything I could to shut things down since I realized it might not all be imaginary."

The sheriff shook his head, trying to comprehend dead people and loved ones at risk because some kids had confused fantasy and reality in a twisted amusement.

"I promise you, none of the guys thought we were involved in more than an elaborate game. Cole? He must know by now, being in the position he is. But he's our genius. And even if he should have known all this was real, I think he just got caught up in the challenge of making it work."

"Just a kids' game," the sheriff said.

"Well, Billy started it. Got a relative in Tucson to provide the front money. If it's real, Billy has to know it. And his daddy and the people here backing the ethanol plant—they'd have known some of it. That must be why Billy set this trap for you. To give them time to make a run for the Caribbean and those numbered accounts before everything comes apart."

"Why leave Cole at such risk?"

"Jealousy. Billy invented the game, got the money from Arizona to start things, but it took Cole to make it really work. I don't think Billy ever forgave him for that. Their dad, he doesn't know about this part. He thinks Cole's spending the night at my place. And, probably, that Cole's too young to be in serious trouble and can just join them later."

"Where is the supervisor? Where are Billy and Dana and the rest of them?"

"The ethanol company keeps a Cessna jet parked in the shed at the airport."

Buffalo Springs' airport consisted of a bladed north-south strip where half a dozen local farmers kept small planes. No tower, no lights, nothing more than some flat ground and a tattered windsock. Lots of flat ground, actually.

"All of us but Cole and Billy just worked on pieces of the game. I did elections. Kevin moved money. Isaac looked for hit men and clients. That leaves you just one person who knows how everything fits together," Ball said. "One who might stop our assassin, if he's still out there trying for a kill."

"Cole?" the sheriff said, knowing it couldn't be anyone else.

"Yes, sir."

"Which means I've got to navigate a mine field and get him off that porch, only you don't know where the mines are or you'd have gotten him loose yourself."

"Yup. I only got here in time to see Billy and Dana plant the last one."

"And where was that, Frank?"

"Well, sir, I'm sorry to tell you that it's right about where you're standing."

◇◇◇

Mad Dog knew this had to be the time. Parker and Matus were in the building, headed into a trap. Hailey was here too, and equally at risk. He tensed some muscles, relaxed them, and found that they'd responded. A little sluggishly, but it wasn't like he could take more time to let them recover. It had to be now.

The detective was way beyond his reach, perched up in the stairwell where he had a clear view of Mad Dog. The uniformed officers had positioned themselves on either side of him as if he were a dangerous suspect they'd just put on the floor but hadn't gotten around to cuffing. They weren't really watching him because they weren't afraid of him. Their eyes shifted back and forth between the ramp and the stair case. What they feared was who or what might come from one of those places. If Mad Dog's muscles responded as well as he hoped, he could probably get to one of them before the other shot him. Or tasered him. Or simply knocked him over the head. And if none of those things happened, the guy in the stairwell could take him out. But it wouldn't let them stay quiet. Interrupting the stillness required for their impending trap was the only thing he had going for him. If he made trouble, made some noise, he might spoil their plans…. Or make them more effective by bringing his rescuers running.

"Damn!" Mad Dog thought the curse had only been in his mind at first. Then he realized the cops were looking at each other, trying to figure out who'd uttered the oath. And the one on the level above had a finger to his lips.

His body had failed to work for so long that Mad Dog hadn't considered simply shouting. His voice would carry well. The building was unnaturally silent. He couldn't hear anyone climbing those stairs. He couldn't hear Hailey clawing concrete. All he could hear were the two cops beside him, breathing hard, excited, anticipating the kill. That and another car. Coming fast—faster than the last one. Fast enough for its tires to break loose on turns. It was right outside. He heard brakes, a thump, the splintering sound of someone driving through one of the wooden gates down at street level. He didn't have a clue who this might be, but apparently still more company was coming to his execution.

"What the…?" one of the uniforms whispered. The other shrugged, and then broke into one of the least welcoming smiles Mad Dog had ever seen.

"Sergeant Parker," he said, turning to the stairwell. "Look what we just bagged."

Parker's head emerged above the level of the concrete floor. So did her gun. There was no sign of Matus yet. Or Hailey. But tires howled down below as someone circled the building, taking corners as fast as they could. The detective directly above Parker leaned down, aiming.

"Trap!" Mad Dog screamed, launching himself toward the nearest of the two uniforms. "Above. On the stairs."

Mad Dog scrambled and somehow put a shoulder into one of them just as Hailey, inexplicably came down the ramp instead of up it. She closed her jaws on the other cop's thigh. Her timing was perfect. He was the one with the functional taser and he'd been about to give Mad Dog yet another dose. Hailey spoiled his aim. As the cop Mad Dog was tackling stuck his pistol in Mad Dog's face, the taser darts missed and caught the officer instead. The man fired, but his shot only deafened Mad Dog instead of tearing a small hole in his face and a big one in the back of his head.

More shots. From the stairs this time. Two of them, Mad Dog thought. With his new hearing problem he couldn't be sure that one shot had really sounded different than the other.

Hailey had changed grips on the second cop. She took the taser out of his gun hand and didn't do his fingers any good in the process. Mad Dog freed himself from the unfortunate shock victim and wheeled and threw a vicious right into Hailey's cop's belly. And missed entirely, falling over and rolling away. Hailey put her feet on one cop's chest and pushed the guy over his partner's back.

Another shot raised sparks and sent cement chips spraying. One bit Mad Dog's cheek. Another opened a ropy vein on the back of his hand. He turned in time to see the third cop, the detective, aiming his way. And then the man disappeared behind the fender of a huge black vehicle. The door flew open and a trim little man in black slacks and matching knit top yelled, "Get in."

There was something familiar about the guy, but another shot whined off the car's hood and reminded Mad Dog he was still a potential target. He did as he was told while looking around for Hailey. She was no where to be seen, of course. The little guy popped a couple of shots out his window and floored the accelerator. The G-forces from under the hood threw Mad Dog back against his seat and slammed the door behind him. The wheels bumped over a couple of objects. Mad Dog couldn't remember there being anything but flat cement. Except, perhaps, the cops who'd intended to kill him.

The SUV slewed around the next bend and the little man began firing toward the detective as they passed the staircase on the opposite side.

There were other shots, too. It was like the OK Corral in here, only more so.

The driver returned his attention to the next corner and suddenly Mad Dog recognized him.

"You're him. The one from the Yaqui village. You're the man who killed that policeman."

"Yeah. And I'm the guy who just saved your life."

Mad Dog was still trying to decide how to react to that when the rear end went loose as they rounded the next corner. The plain-clothes detective was straight ahead of them, running hard for another staircase at the far end of the building. The detective skidded to a stop, threw himself into a shooter's stance, and fired two rounds. One starred the glass in front of the driver. The second did the same in front of Mad Dog.

"Good thing Bobby Earl Macklin likes to bulletproof his personal vehicle."

Mad Dog didn't know a Bobby Earl, though he recalled some Macklins back in Kansas.

"If you want to thank him, he's in the back seat."

Mad Dog started to turn but the little guy hit the accelerator again. Mad Dog peered around the wounded windshield just in time to see the detective come bouncing over the hood and end up spread against the glass.

The driver threw open his door, leveled his gun at the broken man who'd just tried to kill them, and demanded, "Where's Dempsey?"

"We should stop this," Mad Dog said, turning to Macklin for assistance.

Macklin looked back vacantly. That was all he could do. He had no arms, no legs, and no body. He was just a severed head, securely belted into place so he wouldn't roll around back there like some bloody melon.

"Urk," Mad Dog said.

Macklin, of course, did not reply.

◇◇◇

"Well," English said, "obviously I'm not on the mine you saw Billy plant. And if I've already walked on it, it's a dud."

Frank Ball didn't encourage him. "All the ones we set off worked just fine."

The sheriff looked around his feet and his walker. Winter-killed grass was all he saw. Well, maybe a little disturbed dirt way over to his right, in the edge of the headlight's beams. And there, wasn't that clump of grass askew? Maybe the Macklins had gophers—though this wasn't gopher season.

"No sign of one near me. The lawn should be disturbed where anyone planted one of those things."

"Yes, sir," Ball said. "Billy had a military style trenching tool. I'd think you'd see some sign 'cause it seemed like he was working in a hurry."

"I can't stand here forever. Guess I'll just move ahead real slow and stay in the headlights."

"Real slow, sir. I'm sure there's one awful close to where you are."

English shifted his walker a foot forward and followed it, head down and eyes glued to the ground.

"Wait, Sheriff," Ball said. "Look at Cole."

The boy on the porch was waving his hands like crazy again. When the sheriff looked at him, the boy kept his left hand up like he intended the sheriff to stay where he was. Cole's right hand closed, holding up one finger, and slowly lowered to point right at the sheriff. Well, not right at, English decided, but just in front.

And then he saw it. The lawn dipped a little there. A batch of dead leaves lay in a hollow and covered freshly turned earth.

"I see it," the sheriff said. "Does that mean you know where all of them are, Cole?"

The boy's right hand went up again, this time displaying a finger and thumb in a circle with the other three fingers raised. The sheriff had gotten it right.

"So you can direct me? Get me to that porch so I can cut you free?"

The boy made the sign again.

The sheriff took a deep breath and hoped Cole's memory and eyesight were both excellent. "Let's get to it then. People may be dying in Tucson."

Cole pointed to the sheriff's left.

"You want me to move that way?"

Cole circled thumb and finger again. English edged the way the boy indicated, slow and easy, and taking lots of time to examine the ground for himself. It was possible, the sheriff knew, that Cole's real loyalty remained with his brother, even if he had tied him up and left him behind. It was possible Cole had shown him one mine because Frank knew it was there. And that the boy was now directing him straight toward one Frank Ball knew nothing about.

◇◇◇

Heather jumped rails. There was a train station on her left, dark and closed—no surprise in a country where passenger rail service was as uncommon as a night without violence. As if to reinforce her thought, shots echoed from the buildings ahead of her.

The shots would have prompted her to run faster but, even with the aid of a nearly full moon, it was hard to maneuver across the tracks without stumbling.

There was more construction just west of the station, another chain link fence like the one on the side she'd come from. Someone had cut some strands and dug a way under this one, too. She ducked, avoided snagging her clothes, and came out sprinting.

Across the way, headlights wheeled at an impossible angle. And then she realized they were shining out of an upper level from a parking garage. More shots exploded inside the same structure.

A big white Ford idled at one side of the garage. The man inside held a microphone in one hand. He had to be a cop. The generic Ford four-door confirmed it—too big and expensive for any buyer other than government to purchase without investing in a trim package.

The man at the wheel was watching the building and there were sirens, now, coming from every direction. He hadn't noticed her approach. He jumped when she threw herself against his window and put her badge in his face.

"Deputy English," she said, purposefully omitting her jurisdiction. "Mad Dog in there?"

"He is." The guy was too shocked not to answer. Or too guilty about waiting out here where it was safe. "I've got backup on the way."

"Who else is in there?"

"Some of my officers. A Sewa policeman. And whoever just drove that Mercedes SUV inside."

"I'm going in," Heather said, acutely aware that she was carrying nothing more lethal than a pink pocket knife. "You coming with me?"

"No, wait," he said. "You can't go in. You're that Kansas girl, that sheriff's daughter, aren't you? The one we've been looking for all night."

Heather didn't bother answering. There were no entrances on this side of the building and the cop in the Ford had nodded his head to the west when he mentioned the Mercedes. He sounded more likely to hinder her than help. She sprinted for the next corner.

"Hey! You!! Halt!!!"

The Ford started up behind her, burned rubber. She found the corner and went around it. A Mercedes SUV hurtled out an exit, got sparks as it careened off the far curb, and accelerated hard going south. The Ford rounded the corner behind her and a familiar figure came running from the exit the Mercedes had taken.

"Matus," she yelled. "Is my uncle all right?"

The Ford squealed to a halt, blocking the sidewalk in front of her. The man behind the wheel was pointing a service revolver her way, but she hardly noticed.

"I don't know," Matus said. "Your uncle was on the floor up there. Then we got ambushed. That Mercedes came in. The driver killed some cops. He just left. And he took Mad Dog with him."

"Cops? Dead? Who?" The guy in the Ford had lost all interest in Heather.

"Two uniforms. Don't know their names. The Mercedes ran down another, a plain-clothes detective."

"And Sergeant Parker?" the man in the Ford asked.

"She's with the detective. Trying to keep him alive until the EMTs get here." Matus leaned down, peered into the Ford. "Why, it's Chief Dempsey, isn't it?"

"Deputy Chief," Dempsey said, as if he was trying to distance himself from all responsibility.

"That detective had a message for you. Said the guy in the Mercedes wants to meet you at El Tiradito."

"El Tiradito?" Heather and Dempsey made the question a chorus.

"Right. God knows why, but he said he'd have something special for you at the Wishing Shrine."

"Mad Dog?" Heather wondered.

"I'll send every unit I've got," Dempsey said, reaching for the radio.

"No," Matus said. He stuck his gun in the Ford's window and put it in Dempsey's ear. Reached in and tore the microphone out of the chief's hand. Out of its socket, too. Took Dempsey's pistol and threw it across the street. "He said you were to come alone. But I figure he'll put up with the girl and me if we make sure you don't bring anyone else."

◇◇◇

Mad Dog was still trying to figure out what to do about the killer—or maniac, perhaps—as the Mercedes wove between buildings and avoided the swarm of cop cars that seemed to be headed for the place they'd just left. He still hadn't come up with anything when the driver squealed to a stop at the curb near a Mexican restaurant south of some big, sprawling buildings surrounded by limited access parking. There was a small, nearly vacant lot there. It contained only a few modest lamps and clusters of votive candles in niches and on crude candelabras in front of a grimy adobe wall.

"Behold, El Tiradito," the killer said.

"What is it?" Mad Dog asked. He was genuinely curious, but he also felt the power of the place. He nearly forgot he was in the company of a man who'd brought along a severed head.

The killer opened his door and went to the back, removing Macklin from the web of seat belts.

"Shaman like you," the killer said, "I'm surprised you don't know."

"This place is close to the spirit world," Mad Dog said. "I can feel that."

The man with the spare head smiled. "That's hardly a convincing display of your powers at this point."

He carried the head around the front of the SUV and into the lot. For some reason, Mad Dog got out of the Mercedes and followed him. Running like hell would have been smarter, but the guy had saved him at the parking garage. Besides, his own muscles still ached and threatened to cramp because of the mistreatment they'd received earlier. And, for some strange reason, he didn't feel he was in any serious danger from this man.

"The Spanish name, El Tiradito, means the castaway. People also call this place the Wishing Shrine." He nodded at a plaque a few yards in front of a wax-soaked adobe wall and all those flickering candles.

"This is one of those folk shrines you find in this part of the world. They say, a long time ago a young man went searching for his bride and found her in the arms of another man. He killed his rival with an ax, then was put to death for the crime and buried here in unconsecrated ground. Actually, near here.

The city moved him to put in a sewer. But by then, people had taken to lighting candles at his grave. Sometimes, miraculous things happened as a result—cures, wealth, children for the childless—good luck of all sorts. The people who come here do so to make wishes. They say this poor devil, as penitence for what he did, intercedes with God on their behalf. That's what all these candles are. Wishes."

"I've heard of stuff like this," Mad Dog said. "But, how do you know about it, and why have you brought me here?" He wasn't sure he really wanted an answer to that last part.

The killer laughed. "I've got lots of people who do research for me. I was looking for an appropriate place for Bobby Earl, and I feel some sympathy for the poor bastard who's buried here. What I found out about this place makes it perfect. Bobby Earl's head will make a lot of his political opponents' wishes come true. And the message it sends his friends will come with a dramatic postmark."

There was a kind of niche in the adobe wall, a spot where you might expect to find the statue of a saint or maybe a crucifix. A couple of votive candles were all it held. The man with the head, carrying it by the hair, stepped up to the wall, nudged the candles gently aside, and tried placing Bobby Earl in the niche. The ledge was too narrow or too slanted. The head toppled onto more candles below, mixing blood with the wax that had stained this earth for generations. Its hair was singed and smoking a little when the killer picked it back up.

"Uh, why would this man's head answer wishes? And what kind of message will it send?"

The killer patted the hair until it stopped smoking and brushed the face clean, not that Mad Dog could see that doing either made any improvement to its looks. The killer stepped back and examined the wall and the metal rack of candles in front of it.

"Bobby Earl Macklin was a big man in Tucson. Owned car dealerships, restaurants, construction companies that build ticky-tack housing developments that fall apart in a few years and where every place looks alike. Bobby Earl's worth was in the hundreds of millions, maybe more. And he happens to be a cousin to the Macklins you know back in Kansas. Those Macklins don't like you very much, do they?"

"I suppose not," Mad Dog said.

"Bobby Earl's the head, you should pardon the expression, of the local business mafia and their bought and paid for politicos who run this town. And he's the guy who hired me to get you labeled a cop killer and see that you were gunned down by the local constabulary."

"But why? I've never heard of him."

"A favor for his cousins, and it seems you were a thorn in his side anyway."

"Oh?"

"One of those Kansas cousins put together a batch of computer hackers. They persuaded Bobby Earl and his Tucson buddies to come up with the seed money to fund their start up in exchange for fixing a Tucson election. The Kansas Macklins also offered a spot in the middle of nowhere to stick an ethanol plant where Bobby Earl and his pals could launder cash and provide a convenient excuse for their cousin's sudden wealth. Your ruckus over the ethanol plant put you in Bobby Earl's way. By then, the Kansas hackers were arranging for people to clean up little problems like that. They contracted with me for this Tucson operation. Turned me into their Mr. Fix It."

For a moment, Mad Dog thought he'd said Fig Zit, and recalled how the man's features resembled those of the towering monster that had turned so much of his play time in War of Worldcraft into a nightmare.

"Tucson's election hack was coming undone. Some people were considering talking. One of them was your victim at Pascua. He was nobody, just part of Macklin's muscle. But he and the guy who actually fixed the vote got scared and tried to cut a deal. Fick, what your hackers called themselves, had been planning to eliminate you. They broke into your email account and discovered you were on a last minute trip to Tucson. So Bobby Earl and his boys decided to kill three birds with one stone. Me, I was their stone. Even though this thing got complicated and amateurish toward the end, everything would have worked if I hadn't gotten hurt. That's when they decided you'd be easy to take out and they didn't need me anymore.

"I don't understand," Mad Dog confessed.

"Don't need to." The killer moved a couple of candles and tried the head on the metal rack. It looked impressive there, surrounded by glimmering saints, virgins, and images of a very Caucasian Jesus painted on the glass candle containers.

"They underestimated me," the killer said, admiring the way Bobby Earl stared into eternity with a puzzled smile. "So I decided to cut their organization off at the neck," he grinned, "literally."

Mad Dog understood that part.

"Got the head. Now we're waiting for the hands—the guy who's in charge of their local muscle. Handles the dirty work, or arranges for others to do it for him."

"Who's that? Why would he come here?"

"He's the Deputy Chief of Police. Guy named Dempsey. And he'll come because he knows, if he doesn't stop me now, I'll end his gravy train."

"Why won't he just send some of that muscle to gun you down?"

The killer adjusted Bobby Earl's head slightly. "Because I've already taken out most of the people he could use. Even in a city as corrupt as Tucson, there are only so many people willing to kill for you. Fewer, once things start coming apart. And, since they are, Dempsey has to worry that I'd tell them something they could use against him. No. Dempsey has two choices. Come for me, or run."

"And me? Why am I here?" At last, the question Mad Dog had been avoiding.

"I don't know. Just seems right, somehow. This whole bungled mess started with you. Macklin and Dempsey, and the Kansas Macklins, have been using me to set you up to get killed since you got here. With the tables turned, maybe I owe you the pleasure of seeing one of the men who tried to kill you die."

"Then what?"

"Then I go after Fick."

Headlights rounded the corner north of them and a large unmarked Ford pulled in behind the Mercedes.

"But first things first," the killer said. "Dempsey's here."

◇◇◇

The sheriff was surprised to find the last two mines so close to the porch. Their tripwires were strung where they would be disturbed by anyone taking the most natural paths to rescue young Cole. Considering that they were designed so a small explosive charge propelled them above the ground to a height where they would cause maximum damage to surrounding troops, there wasn't much chance Cole would have survived if anyone set off either of them.

And finally the sheriff was past them, safely on the porch. Duct tape was wrapped clear around the boy's head. The sheriff used his pocket knife to saw through the tape and was none too gentle when he peeled it away from Cole's mouth.

"Can you put a stop to what's going on in Tucson?" English asked.

"Not without a computer. Maybe not even then."

"Why?"

"Our assassin's running himself," Cole said. "He knows we tried to shut him down. Now, the best I can do is find him and put together a strike force to take him out."

Cold words. The boy was talking about a man's life. Cole was what, fifteen maybe?

"Frank," the sheriff shouted. "Can you put Cole's computer and this house back on line?"

"No, sir. I blew the cable where it comes out of town and then wrecked their satellite dish. No way to get on from here."

"Where's the nearest working computer?"

"Billy," Cole said. "My brother's got a satellite phone link for his laptop. We could use that."

The sheriff shook his head. "Airport's just down the road. In the time it took me to cross your lawn, Billy could have driven to and from there half a dozen times. They've had plenty of time to leave."

"They're waiting for me," Cole said. "Billy told me. This is just a trial I have to pass. A way to make me prove I'm worthy by stopping you and getting loose to join them."

"A trial?" The sheriff lost it. "You were supposed to let me get killed. Jesus, kid. People died because of you tonight. This is real, not some stupid quest out of a computer game."

Cole shook his head. "I kept you safe, and Billy wouldn't actually leave me."

"Look, Sheriff, I know it's real," Cole said. "But only sort of. Billy set it up so we use paintball guns and cherry bombs instead of the real thing. I don't know why Ed would…"

"Are those real mines or firecrackers you just walked me through?"

"Real. We get some of the real stuff to play with now and then. I thought that was weird, when Billy and his girlfriend planted them. But then I figured they were probably disarmed."

"What if we really fixed elections?" Frank said from the driveway. "What if the money we transferred is real, or our assassin hasn't been playing paintball tag? I was in town, Cole. Ed Miller didn't use a cherry bomb. He's really and truly dead."

"But, Billy…."

"Shut up, kid," the sheriff said. He laid the boy's Adirondack over on its side facing the house, then he tipped over a redwood table and shoved it between the boy and the yard. It would be a long shot for a sawed-off, but at least a shotgun had the advantage of throwing lots of lead. He picked a target.

"Frank," the sheriff said. "Duck your head around the far side of the house for a minute."

"Already have, sir."

The sheriff crouched behind his fortification, sighted, and pulled the trigger. The night lit with fire. The sheriff's headlights and windshield blew out. Chips of wood and broken glass from the house rained on them as the sheriff bent and got in Cole's face.

"Was that mine disarmed? How do you survive the trial your brother set for you if I trip a mine anywhere near this porch? That shrapnel would have torn the life out you, boy, and you know it."

Cole didn't answer this time. Instead, his eyes got large and filled with tears. He began to whimper.

"Could Billy or that laptop still be at the airport?" the sheriff called to Frank.

"No, sir. I don't think so. Billy's a better pilot than Mr. Macklin. None of the others were checked out to fly a jet, not that I know of. Most likely, the nearest computer is the one Mrs. Kraus has back in Doc Jones' office."

The sheriff sawed through the tape binding Cole's legs and started on his hands. "Then we'll hightail it back to town. Put Cole on the internet and see if we can find out what's going on. What we can do to help. And I can get out some kind of alert on that plane."

"You don't have to do that, sir. Look east."

The sheriff stopped cutting duct tape long enough to glance toward Frank, then beyond him, across the farm yard and the stock pens beyond. Dawn was close. He hadn't even noticed, but you could see the infinite horizon out there, backlit where the sun would soon rise.

"What?" the sheriff said. And then he saw it. A cloud of thick smoke climbed the endless sky, its source hidden behind a distant row of Osage Orange trees. Two, maybe three miles past the airport, he guessed. "Is that…?" he started to ask Frank.

"Yes, sir. I borrowed one of the mines before Billy and Dana set them out here. Right after I came to the office…when I realized this might be real."

"You rigged an explosive device on that Cessna, Frank?"

"I did, sir. I got one of those mines and went to the airport and put it where, if they took off and raised the landing gear…."

Frank Ball began to cry, too. "I didn't think they'd actually go. In spite of everything, I still thought this had to be a game. But, if it was real, I knew they'd take that plane and…."

"My God," the sheriff said. "You blew them out of the sky?"

"Yes, sir," Frank said with a forlorn little chuckle. "In our game, Billy would have had to give me extra points for pulling a successful coup d'état."

◇◇◇

Heather was the first one out of the car. Matus had provided directions, and kept his pistol in Dempsey's gut to make sure the assistant chief didn't interfere.

"Like the Energizer Bunny," the psycho quipped. "You keep coming and coming, don't you?"

"Are you all right?" Heather asked Mad Dog. Her uncle was her first concern.

"I'm fine, thank you," the psycho said, playing with her.

Mad Dog nodded and she turned her attention back to the strange man who'd planned to mutilate her, then briefly turned into a partner of convenience.

"And, thanks to me, your uncle is fine, too. As you can see," he waved a hand toward the rack of candles beside him, "I found Bobby Earl Macklin. We had an interesting discussion about the ethics of fixing elections, then turning on the people you employ to clean up the resulting mess…until he lost his head."

Heather had thought it was some kind of gargoyle-like decoration—part of this odd, open-air holy place—a piñata, maybe. But a second glance told her it was real. That was the face she'd seen on the billboard and in the photograph on the dead doctor's desk. A wave of nausea swept her and, if the psycho hadn't been watching, she might have doubled over and vomited in the street. Instead, she did her best to hide any reaction. If she paled, the lighting here wasn't good enough for him to notice.

Matus climbed out of the other side of the Ford, pistol at his side. It took the psycho's attention away from her and she brushed cold sweat from her forehead.

"Another surprise," the psycho said. "I hate to complain, Captain, but I was hoping for Chief Dempsey instead."

"He's here," Matus said, "but I don't think he wants to get out of the car."

"He didn't come voluntarily, then?" the psycho asked.

"No more than Mr. Macklin," Matus said, "though he's kept himself more together."

The psycho laughed. "Perhaps I can correct that. Ask the chief to step out here and join us, won't you?"

Matus had told Heather about this place on the way over. It had sounded quaint and intriguing. Bobby Earl Macklin's head and the psycho's presence transformed it into something bizarre, like a set from a bad horror movie.

"Why?" she asked. "I think, rather than meet you, Chief Dempsey might prefer to turn state's evidence."

"A deputy chief of police probably wouldn't do well in prison," the psycho replied. "That's one reason. The other is I have a gun, too," and he did, though Heather wasn't quite sure how the thing suddenly appeared in his hand. "If Dempsey doesn't get out of the car, I'll use it to kill your uncle."

"In which case," Matus said, raising his pistol, "I'd kill you."

"Don't be too sure, Captain. I'm extraordinarily good at my profession, as you probably know by now, and that includes killing people and preventing them from killing me."

It all sounded very macho, but Heather knew he wasn't bragging. "Get out," she told Dempsey, and he did, though she couldn't understand why. Maybe it was because the chief believed this man, too. Maybe Dempsey hoped he could buy his way out of this. Or maybe he believed waiting in the car only delayed his certain death—together with Matus' and Mad Dog's and hers, as well.

Heather remembered the five stages her mother had gone through when she learned her cancer would be fatal—denial, anger, bargaining, depression, and acceptance. Dempsey must have rushed through the first two on the way from the parking garage.

"You're a professional," the chief said before he cleared the door. On Heather's side, she noticed, so maybe he was still clinging to a little denial, keeping the car between him and the psycho. "You don't kill for pleasure. You kill for money. That means you must be willing not to kill, as well, if the price is right. So tell me what you want. I'll see it's paid."

The psycho smiled a peculiar smile and Heather thought Dempsey was wrong about the man killing only for profit. The psycho enjoyed his work. She started around the front of the Ford, hands raised to show she wasn't a threat.

"Look," she said. "You've had your revenge. You got the man who ordered your death. Give us my uncle and step back and enjoy a stretched out version of Dempsey's suffering—public humiliation, the courts, prison. Do that, and you can walk away from here." She dangled the Ford's keys. "Drive, actually, in a Tucson police car. And that's probably the only way you can get away from this spot, even if you kill all of us. They'll be looking for Macklin's SUV, and downtown is crawling with police. Some of them are probably on their way here by now."

The night was filled with sirens but the psycho's shrug was casual. "You're right, I suppose." He met her at the front of the unmarked police car.

"Ten million, Dempsey. If I don't get it I'll come back and...."

He snatched the keys with his bad hand and dodged the flying kick she launched, catching her other leg at the knee with a leg sweep that dropped her like a stone. His gun went off at the same time and when she looked up he had managed to get to Matus and disarm him. The psycho's pistol pushed against the captain's temple.

No one else had moved. Mad Dog looked dazed. Dempsey just stood in the street. He seemed shocked. The disbelief phase, maybe, since he slowly raised his hands to his stomach and looked down at the bloody horror he found there.

Matus tried to throw an elbow and there was a moment when Heather thought she could rush the psycho. It was over before she managed to get to her feet. The psycho smiled and shook his head and she knew she couldn't do a thing to him before he killed her and Matus. And Mad Dog, who, by then, would be trying to tear the psycho limb from limb with his bare hands, no matter what the odds.

"I should probably eliminate you all," the psycho said. "But you've been a big help to me, Heather. I owe you for Bobby Earl and Dempsey, and now the car."

His knee lifted off Matus' back and the gun left the captain's temple. The psycho started around the Ford to where Dempsey now sat in the middle of the street, watching blood well from between his fingers. Three steps from the door, the psycho froze. Heather didn't understand why, at first. And then she knew what he'd heard, even over the symphony of sirens that filled downtown. It was Hailey's throaty growl.

◇◇◇

Mad Dog wasn't surprised. Nothing Hailey did surprised him anymore. Including, seeming to materialize here at the shrine as if by magic.

"Call off your wolf," the killer said. "I don't want to have to shoot her."

"I can't tell her what to do," Mad Dog said. "And I don't think you have to worry about shooting her. You're fast, but she's greased lightning."

Hailey growled again. She had crept closer to the killer, past Heather. No one else had moved and Mad Dog thought that was a good idea.

"I think she wants everyone to stay where they are," Mad Dog said. "And Mr. Whoever-You-Are, I think she wants you to drop your gun."

"Won't happen," the killer said. Had he pivoted just a little? Hadn't the gun been down at his side a moment ago, not at his belt, its muzzle tracking toward Hailey? "I'm getting in this car and leaving and I'll shoot anyone or anything that tries to stop...."

The gun came around fast. Hailey rose from the ground like a missile and hit the killer in the throat. The gun might have reached Hailey if Heather hadn't gotten to if just before it exploded. A bullet scored the Ford's roof and went screaming into the night. Killer, niece, and wolf tumbled onto the street behind the Ford and Mad Dog vaulted the vehicle's hood as Matus ran around the trunk. Dempsey just sat in the street and bled.

By the time Mad Dog cleared the Ford, it was over. Heather had relieved the killer of his gun. Hailey had the man by the neck, though she hadn't clamped her jaws tight. Not yet. The killer was on hands and knees. No matter how efficient he might be at dealing death, he seemed to understand he couldn't hurt Hailey before her teeth severed arteries, veins, windpipe—maybe even spinal cord.

Heather put a little distance between herself and the killer. Mad Dog stepped back as Hailey suddenly pulled away, pausing for one quick nip before trotting to Mad Dog's side. Something hung from her mouth. He bent and took it. It was his medicine bundle.

The killer slowly climbed to his feet. He still had the keys to the Ford in one hand. "I won't let you take me in," he said. "I'm leaving in this car now. That or you'll kill me."

"Hailey's right," Mad Dog said. "Let him go. We don't need to kill him."

"Just cripple him," Matus said. "Blow off a kneecap."

Mad Dog held up a hand. "No. The only people he's injured here deserved it, more or less. He won't hurt anyone else. Hailey knows that or she would have finished him."

"But...," Matus sputtered.

"You're sure, Uncle Mad Dog?" Heather still had the man covered, but he knew she wanted a reason not to pull the trigger.

"Yeah," Mad Dog said. "I just had a conversation with the spirit of this shrine. Nobody dies here. Nobody else gets hurt. Hey, all of us even get what we want. Except Dempsey."

The killer opened the door, shook his head at such silliness, and put the key in the ignition. "I wished for ten million, you crazy asshole. Am I getting that, too?"

Mad Dog shrugged. "If El Tiradito decides you deserve it."

The man laughed, but there was a hollow sound to it. The Ford roared to life, smoked tires, and disappeared into the night.

"Shit," Matus said. "We should have stopped him." He had his phone out and was dialing 911.

"No," Heather said. "I don't think so. Crazy as it seems, I trust Hailey and Uncle Mad Dog on this one."

"Maybe," Matus said, then paused to tell an emergency operator they needed an ambulance right now at the Wishing Shrine.

"Anyway," Matus told Heather, "that was impressive. The way you disarmed him. I know you're about to become a lawyer, but if you ever change your mind and want a job in law enforcement...."

A marked police unit careened around the corner and squealed to a stop. Doors flew open and two officers came out behind them, guns drawn, shouting instructions.

Heather tossed her weapon away before they were out of the car, refrained from reaching for her badge, and raised her hands. "Deputy sheriff," she shouted. She nodded toward Matus and added, "Tribal police."

"This what you wished for, old man?" Matus asked Mad Dog as they followed the officers' orders and lay face down in the street.

"Can't tell you," Mad Dog said. "Otherwise it might not come true."

◇◇◇

Mrs. Kraus opened the door to the sheriff's office. The electricity was on, just like the man from the rural electric company had assured her. The ceiling lights glowed, though with the sun up for a good twenty minutes now, they weren't really needed.

The janitor had come in and swept up the shards of broken glass from the windows. He'd even covered the bottom half of one with a clear plastic sheet. The rest were open to the chill air that left her producing little clouds with every breath.

Mrs. Kraus didn't take off her heavy coat when she sat at her desk and picked up a phone. The dial tone was back. That was why she'd abandoned their temporary headquarters at Doc's office. The phone company never had managed to switch the sheriff's calls over to Doc's. That meant someone had to be here. There were lots of loose ends still out there, waiting to be cleaned up.

She fired up her computer. It came on, none the worse for the explosion except for a dusty screen. She got a cloth out of her drawer and wiped it down. The little blue bar at the bottom of her monitor told her it was 7:51 a.m. Hell, she wasn't even supposed to be in the office yet and she'd already put in at least half a day's work. And not slept a wink.

Sheriff English was out with Doc and the volunteer fire department, pulling the remains of Billy Macklin and Dana Miller, and pretty much every member of the Benteen County Board of Supervisors, out of the wreckage of the ethanol company's corporate jet. Just for the hell of it, she logged back onto War of Worldcraft.

Mad Dog's character was right where she'd left it, standing over the corpse of the once mighty Fig Zit. Recalling the host of upgrades the WOW tech had piled on this character, she decided to take a stroll through the waterfall trees. She soon found an epic fire demon in the mouth of a nearby cave. He hit her with a fire bolt the moment she stepped out of the mist. She charged, swinging the new infinity ax Madwulf had been given. One blow and the demon went down. And there, behind him, was a treasure chest. She dropped her ax and picked up the chest as a familiar voice sent a chill arcing down her spine.

"Good morning, Mrs. Kraus."

She worked her keyboard and made Madwulf whirl. There was Fig Zit, huge and threatening, blocking the entrance to the cave.

"We haven't met," the monster said, "but Heather and Mad Dog will know who I am. If they wonder how I got on your computer tell them I hired another internet firm to hack into Fick's. They told me how Billy Macklin and his friends have been using this game to mess with you and Mad Dog and they got me access to this character."

Mrs. Kraus was too frightened to understand a thing he was saying.

"Tell Heather and Mad Dog I got my wish. I used my contacts to bribe my way through a border gate into Mexico, though we didn't get everyone paid off. After the shoot out, the car they gave me was a flaming wreck. I traded it for an idling three-quarter ton truck that someone abandoned during the gunfight. And I seem to have gotten clear with. It's equipped with everything, including a computer with a satellite link. That left me wondering what was back in the enclosed bed. U.S. Federal Reserve Notes. Counterfeit, though, and useless to me, but the face value should be…. Well, Mad Dog already knows that."

His words refused to register right then. She'd let go of her ax to pick up the treasure chest and left herself defenseless.

"They may be interested to know what Fick means. It's more than a play on words—you know, Fig Zit, Fix It, Fick's I.T. And it's not just a naughty word in German. It's an acronym. Billy Macklin called his fake internet technology company FICK for Frank, Isaac, Colin, and Kevin. Get it?"

Not a word. The monster was back and it had trapped her. She did the only thing she could think of. She threw the chest at him. He dodged it and smiled.

"But none of that has anything to do with why I decided to pay you a visit, Mrs. Kraus. I've had time to think about what happened this morning. Tell Heather she's the closest I've ever come to matching myself against an equal. The idea of doing that again, once she's ready…. Well, it excites me. So, tell her to continue preparing herself. When the time is right, I'll be back."

The Fig Zit figure began to come apart in front of Mrs. Kraus like some cartoon character. Which, come to think of it, he was. He broke into thousands of pieces and they ran around like crazy, making whistling noises as the air rushed out of them and they shrank away to nothing until she was alone with the waterfall forest and the cave and the newly empowered Madwulf. Alone for now, but he'd said he'd come back.

How could…? Just in case, she logged off. It was cold in the sheriff's office, but her forehead was beaded with sweat.

She sat, for a few minutes, trying to remember all the stuff he'd said. Nonsense, or was it? She reached for a phone to call the WOW tech and find out how Fig Zit had turned up on her screen again. There was no dial tone when she put the handset to her ear. Instead, a familiar voice she was only too happy to hear said, "Hello? Hello? Anybody there?"

"Heather English. Is that really you? Are you all right, child?"

"Fine, Mrs. Kraus. I'm fine. Mad Dog, too. And Hailey. None of us are hurt. We're at Tucson police headquarters and it's finally over. We're all safe. How about there? Is Daddy okay?"

"Sure is, honey."

"I've been trying to get him on his cell but I keep getting his voice mail. I was starting to worry so I called you."

"His batteries ran down. He forgot to put it on the charger last night and he's been using it since Mad Dog's place got bombed."

"Is Dad there? Can I speak to him?"

"No, I'm sorry. He's still working the case. Not that there are any bad guys left for him to chase down. They made a run for it and their plane crashed and the rest of them turned out to be just kids. Nobody left for him…." Mrs. Kraus trailed off long enough to wonder who had just told her about the boy's names. Who was Fig Zit if Englishman really had them all? Who was the ghost in her machine?

"Can you get word to Daddy? Ask him to call me as soon as he can. I'll tell him everything that happened down here. It got pretty wild."

"They catch that hit man who was after you?"

"No, he sort of got away…." She tapered off and muffled voices made happy noises in the background.

"Heather, honey, you still there?"

"You know, I think Uncle Mad Dog was right."

Mrs. Kraus snorted. "Mad Dog is a lot of things, but right ain't usually one of them."

"I don't know, Mrs. Kraus. Pam just ran through the door and threw herself in his arms. That's something he'd wish for."

Mrs. Kraus was not prepared to comment on Mad Dog's love life. Besides, she was still puzzling over this latest Fig Zit appearance. Maybe she should tell Heather about him.

"And," Heather said, "I just decided. Captain Matus can have that new officer he said he wanted."

"You lost me. What are you talking about, honey?"

What Heather said next did nothing to enlighten Mrs. Kraus.

"Maybe that should be Officer Honey. Tell Daddy I said that. Tell him his little girl is going to carry on a family tradition."

Afterword & Acknowledgments

War of Worldcraft is a thinly disguised (and modified for my convenience) version of World of Warcraft (WOW), a massive, multi-player, online, role-playing game It's an amazing place, populated by more than ten million players around the world. I've been running characters there, purely as research for this novel, you understand. Playing is much like watching a high-quality animated movie in which you're one of the characters. Most players are far younger than Mad Dog, Mrs. Kraus, or yours truly, but I suspect more than a few people of a certain age pass among us, unnoticed.

WOW, and games far more violent, are part of the world in which young people grow up today. I don't gank (ambush busy or injured enemies) or corpse sit (wait for recently killed characters to revive at half strength so I can kill them again more easily), yet I've still amassed more than 10,000 kills on player vs. player battlefields (where you earn honor to buy better equipment). To score 10,000 kills, I've probably died at least 30,000 times. At my age, I have no problem understanding the difference between WOW's fantasy world and the real one, but I was young and immortal once. I wonder, if we'd been exposed to so many adventures in which we couldn't die, it might not have led my generation to even more foolish real-life risks than we managed with only books, radio, TV, comics, and movies to inspire us. We took too many, anyway, though most of us survived them. Still, it seems to me the lines are less clear, and families less available to explain things like reality and fantasy to recent generations. I wonder, too, how much longer my research will continue, now that this novel is written. In any case, thanks to a couple of amateurish avatars I abandoned long ago, then to the pair I took to level 70, Borgward and Originalcyn. And to the many helpful avatars and the real people behind them I met along the way—except gankers and corpse sitters, of course.

There actually are allegations that a Pima County election was fixed. Tucson is the county seat. That election was held in May 2006 to establish a regional transportation authority (RTA) and fund it with a half-cent sales tax. To date, nothing is certain, though there is a great deal of circumstantial evidence that indicates a fix may have taken place. Election integrity activists sued when the county refused to release public records—databases the county defined as computer programs. The county lost and recently turned over the largest collection of election databases anywhere in the United States. They are under investigation but have yet to yield a smoking gun.

In case you aren't aware of it, in our rush to fix Florida's hanging chads, we saturated the United States with a series of proprietary software programs that count ballots secretly. The idea of a secret ballot is a hallowed concept in American democracy, but that's voting in secret, not counting in secret. As admitted by experts for both sides in Pima County's RTA election trial, none of the secret election-counting software programs available in the United States are remotely secure. Hacker friendly, is a common term for them—most easily hacked from the inside, which is what is alleged to have happened in Pima County. The simple solution would be to recount the ballots. Nearly everyone on both sides now advocates that. By Arizona law, however, ballots can be physically counted only when an election is decided by 1/10th of 1% or less, or when a criminal investigation takes place. There are two prosecutorial agencies in Arizona with the right to conduct such an investigation. The Pima County Attorney's office, which has been acting as defense attorneys for the accused, is one. The other is the Arizona Attorney General's office. Trouble is, the AAG's office already conducted a careless investigation and cleared the county of wrongdoing. That they did so in a cooperative effort with Pima County (the accused) makes the results suspect. Especially when the outside investigator, hired and partially paid by Pima County, qualified their finding with the following statement: "During testing it was discovered that the GEMS [Global Election Management System] software exhibits fundamental security flaws that make definitive validation of data impossible due to the ease of data and log manipulation from outside the GEMS software itself." In other words, we've got a mess here.

By the time you read this, we may know whether the RTA election was stolen. To find out, use a search engine and enter as key words "Pima County" and "RTA election." If you find the case still hasn't been resolved, I'd suggest keeping a very close eye on the way your own jurisdiction counts votes. It's probably not remotely secure. Or check my website for updates. I'll post status reports between making aluminum foil hats and watching for black helicopters.

In any case, though I loosely based the election hack in this novel on the one alleged to have occurred in Pima County's RTA election, none of the characters in the book should be confused with real people or situations. That goes for the rest of the story as well. With the exception of Hailey, of course.

When you're writing suspense novels, introducing law enforcement officers who can't be trusted is a powerful device. In my own experience, the worst Tucson policeman I've encountered showed me some attitude—good-guy-having-a-bad-day sort of stuff. The rest, the vast majority, have been exemplary public servants, doing a tough job and doing it well.

Phi Beta Kimba, to whom this book is dedicated, was one of the Nisimons I've been lucky enough to share my life with. Nisimon is a Cheyenne term for a personal spirit helper—a familiar, a Hailey. Kimba was part of our German Shepherd herd, the brilliant one who sometimes seemed to think more deeply about life than I am capable of doing. I owe a tremendous debt to all the dogs in my life. I hope I've been worthy of them.

Singer/songwriter/legend John Stewart died while this book was being written. It always felt as if he were writing the lyrics to my life. That's why I've quoted him for epigrams to every book in this series. I can't imagine a world in which he won't continue sharing his astonishing insights. Not that he didn't leave enough to keep me in epigrams as long as I live.

This book would not exist without the immense help and support of my critique group, Elizabeth Gunn, Susan Cummins Miller, William Hartmann, and Margaret Falk (by whatever pen name she may be using). Thanks too, to Jeff Budd, Dr. Karl H. Schlesier, and Maj. Gen. (Ret.) R. James Fairfield, Jr. for reading the manuscript and offering insights. Without Poisoned Pen Press, I would be writing, if at all, for an audience unlikely to include more than a handful of friends. Finally and especially, thanks to Barbara, my personal editor, publicist, and child bride. But for her, the words would not exist.

For insights into Tucson politics and election integrity issues, special thanks to John Brakey, co-founder of Audit-AZ; Attorney William Risner, who won the release of all those election databases; and former Campbell/Grant Northeast Neighborhood Association President, Ken O'Day. I can't say that what they've taught me made me happy, but it's been an education.

For errors, I alone am responsible.

JMH
Tucson, by way of Hutchinson, Partridge, Darlow, Manhattan, Wichita, Sedna Creek, et Tabun, Albuquerque, and a yellow brick road

To receive a free catalog of Poisoned Pen Press titles, please contact us in one of the following ways:

Phone: 1-800-421-3976
Facsimile: 1-480-949-1707
Email: info@poisonedpenpress.com
Website: www.poisonedpenpress.com

Poisoned Pen Press
6962 E. First Ave. Ste. 103
Scottsdale, AZ 85251